# TOGETHER

# TOGETHER

Ellen Roddick

ST. MARTIN'S PRESS
New York

**Library of Congress Cataloging in Publication Data**

Roddick, Ellen.
Together.

I. Title.
PZ4.R6858To        [PS3568.0343]        813'.5'4        78–21362
ISBN 0–312–80768–6

# CONTENTS

# TOGETHER

# 1

# CHANGES

"DIFFICULT as Manhattan can be," said Nina Lathrop to her friend, Gretchen, "I'm always ready to come back from the country by Labor Day."

Gretchen looked around the festive Crystal Room, where they were having lunch. "This restaurant is such a pretty place to celebrate reentry."

Nina frowned at the small bouquet of autumn flowers in the center of the white tablecloth (printed with a flowered border) and wondered how best to phrase her question. Gretchen's face was strained, with a greyish undertone. Nina wanted to find out why, without seeming to be concerned. The last thing you need when you're down, she thought, is someone implying that you look terrible.

"Would you care to order drinks?" asked a young woman dressed in a waiter's black and white uniform.

Nina and Gretchen stared at one another. They did not usually drink at lunch.

Gretchen shrugged. "What the hell? I'll have a glass of white wine."

Nina ordered white wine and soda, for the sake of companionship.

1

Although their fortieth birthdays were not as far in the future as they might have wished, the two women, dressed in fashionable cotton dresses, were not dissatisfied with their appearances.

"I love your hair," said Gretchen. "When did you do that?"

"This summer. I got fed up with trying to cope with it long." Nina ran her fingers through her short auburn curls. "I envy yours being straight."

"It's boring." Gretchen had pinned up her black hair in a neat French twist and wore pearl earrings to relieve the severity of the style. "How was the faculty meeting this morning? Did you like the new headmaster?"

"I'm not sure. He's awfully high powered and intense."

Nina taught kindergarten at the Twickham School. In May, the former headmaster had resigned, protesting the board of directors' veto of his plan to introduce school uniforms (as a symbol of the self-discipline and order that the coeducational student body of kindergarten through twelfth grade increasingly lacked and needed). The board had maintained that students' individuality would be threatened, if the traditional *laissez-faire* policy toward their attire were abandoned in favor of uniformity.

The board had then engaged a prestigious firm of "head-hunters" who, in turn, had produced (among other candidates) Mortimer Bartholomew Hinks, Ph.D. It was evident almost immediately that he was the man for Twickham. Parents and faculty shared the board's relief when he agreed to leave the New England preparatory school, where he had been headmaster for seven years, in favor of the challenge and celebrity offered by Twickham. *The New York Times* had followed in detail the school's crisis, and Nina knew a great deal about Mort Hinks before he arrived.

"He's well-qualified, of course, . . ." she said.

"But?"

"I don't know. He's self-assured without being all that winning. Most of the faculty like him."

"What does he look like?"

"As handsome as his name: Mort Hinks."

Gretchen smiled. "Bitch."

"Short and fair, with wavy, greying blonde hair and a lived-in face. Tortoise-shell glasses."

"Definitely not your type, but so what? You only have to work with him."

"Some women find that type attractive. He has a wife and two kids."

"You're spoiled by being married to David."

"He is devastating."

Nina's husband, a lawyer, was tall and sturdy, with dark hair and eyes. She and David had returned the previous day from their country house in Connecticut, with their two little boys. Gretchen had telephoned her in the country to make this lunch date.

When the drinks had been brought, Nina said, "You've been working hard? And Burt?"

"I've been made a vice-president of the bank."

"Gretchen, that's super!"

"And Burt has disappeared."

Nina's mind blurred and disengaged. "I don't understand."

"Nor do I. Last Friday, his office closed at noon for the holiday, but he didn't come home or phone over the entire Labor Day weekend."

"Did you call the hospitals?"

"I received a telegram on Friday evening, saying, 'I'm okay. Don't try to track me down.' "

"How bizarre. Maybe he's had a nervous breakdown."

"This morning I phoned his office and asked to speak to him. His secretary said he was in conference."

"He's functioning at work?"

"Evidently."

Nina could not think of anything to say.

Gretchen added, "Sometimes I feel as if I'm being black-listed by God."

Nina reached across the table and squeezed her arm. "Your career is successful."

"That's not enough. My marriage is . . ." her laugh was more giddy than bitter. "Shall we say, in trouble? I gave up having babies for Burt's sake."

"I understood his not wanting to start a new family with you. Weren't his kids by his first wife already in college when you married him?"

"Sure, but I wasn't even thirty."

"You can still have a baby."

"With whom?"

"Has he ever done this before?"

"Not bloody likely."

The waitress took their orders: two chef's salads with the dressing on the side.

"I wish I had the window-washing concession here," said Gretchen.

The dining room was enclosed on three sides by floor-to-ceiling glass, letting in sunlight and the greenery of Central Park. Prisms of glass sparkled overhead.

Looking up, Nina said, "Whoever chose these chandeliers understands glass the way Italians understand fountains."

"The ceiling cheers me up, painted in pastels, with all those plaster garlands."

"Actually, ducks, you don't seem all that much in need of cheering up."

Startled, Gretchen thought about it and agreed. "Burt and I have lost touch. The suspense of not knowing where he is or what he's doing is demoralizing, but having him gone isn't half bad. We're both completely involved in our careers."

"Is there another woman?"

"Maybe."

"Don't you care? Do you have a lover?"

"No lover, but I do crave a passionate affair."

"While you're married?"

"Wouldn't you?"

"Never!"

"David must be something special."

"I think so."

"Aren't you a shade smug?"

"The job I want, two darling sons, and a successful husband. It's not perfect."

"Like?"

"Keeping house in Connecticut, as well as in our apartment here, is a hassle."

"You have a housekeeper, Nina."

"There's still plenty of domestic organization and trivia left for me."

"And?"

"David works too hard. He isn't home much."

"And?"

"I'd like to see more of the boys than I do during the school year. Teaching is a full-time job."

"Poor thing."

Nina conceded. "It's a good life. I'm lucky."

"I'm restless."

Their salads were placed before the women who barely moistened the ingredients with the house dressing.

"Excuse me, madam," said the head waiter, suddenly standing over Gretchen. "Your husband is on the telephone. It's against our policy to page, but he says it's an emergency."

Gretchen stood up so quickly that her chair tilted against the man seated behind her. The head waiter righted it and led Gretchen out of the dining room.

Nina put down her fork and surveyed the people around her to distract herself from the anxiety she was feeling. When Gretchen finally returned to the table, her face and eyes were empty. She sat down and began to laugh softly.

"Well what? What?" urged Nina.

"Burt called to say he's left me for another woman. His secretary is coming up to our apartment this afternoon to pack a suitcase for him. He gave her our key."

"You're not serious."

"Could I make up a thing like that? I'm a banker, not a comedienne."

"Was he drunk?"

"Calm and sober. Said he called here to tell me, because he knew I wouldn't make a scene in public. He hates scenes. And of course you'd be with me to help me 'absorb the shock.'"

"He must feel crummy."

"Sounded fine to me."

"He *ought* to feel crummy."

" 'Oughts' have nothing to do with it."

"You were laughing when you sat down."

"His chutzpah is so typical. And I guess I'm, well, relieved. Does that sound callow?"

"Not as callow as his phone call. I'd be frantic."

"You don't know how you'd feel until it happens."

"How did he know that you're here with me?"

"He called my office, and my secretary told him."

They resumed eating their salads, contemplating rather than conversing.

"Is there anything I can do for you?" asked Nina as she poured them each a second cup of coffee. "This situation is astonishing."

"Keep your ear to the ground for a smaller apartment. I'll be moving."

"Occasionally there are apartment rental notices on the bulletin board in the faculty lounge."

"Introduce me to available men."

"I don't know any at the moment."

"What about your new headmaster?"

"I already told you. He's married."

"Too bad."

"Single men will be turning up. People get divorced all the time."

*

Nina, who prided herself on having a well-ordered life, went from what she viewed as a rather surreal luncheon straight to her neighborhood supermarket. She had brought her list with her when she left home that morning. Shopping was a reassuring activity, in the aftermath of her friend's marital drama. Lifting a four-roll package of toilet tissue from the shelf, Nina dropped it into her shopping cart. Today the supermarket offered only two choices in white, and she took what looked like the softer. She never bought colored paper, because when it eventually became sewage and reached rivers and lakes, its dye killed fish. Then she remembered a surprise she had received in a friend's half bath (as real estate ads call a lavatory) and grabbed the package up again, holding it to her nose and sniffing through the plastic wrapping.

"My God. It does stink," she said aloud. "Cheap scent." Frowning, she returned the package to the shelf and took instead four individual rolls of the other leading brand.

Nina continued pushing her cart down the aisle, stopping for dishwasher powder, plastic sandwich bags, and all-purpose cleanser. Absently she checked her shopping list, her mind still on the toilet paper. Why was it perfumed? Would she find it so puzzling and repulsive if it were redolent with, say, Miss Dior? Was it hygienic?

"It probably gives you venereal disease," she said.

A young mother with a toddler riding amidst her groceries glanced up shrewdly and saw not the Big Apple Loony she had expected but a tall slim woman with a strikingly candid face, big brown eyes, and a perfectly peachy complexion. Feigning innocence, Nina looked around as if she, too, wondered where the voice had come from. "I've got to stop talking aloud to myself," she thought. "It's weird. What if that were one of my students' mothers?"

Nina moved on, speculating about Gretchen's future and Burt's present. The media—films, discs, the tube, novels—hard sell the idea that falling in love is wonderful, is to be sought, nourished, and cherished. Nina assumed that everyone except the unabashed cynic and flagrantly disillusioned buys this premise. Yet for most women and men, the time for romantic love is generally (but not always, she realized) during their teens and twenties.

Most married lovers in their thirties and forties or beyond find that romance no longer has top priority. Or so Nina thought. If a mate, a child, a job, disappoints, there may be solace in dalliance. A friend might confess, as Gretchen had, a craving for passion. Engaging in total upheaval, however, as Burt was doing, for the sake of romance (and surely he must be wildly in love with this other woman) was not ordinary in Nina's circle of acquaintances. There were divorces, but they grew out of unhappy marriages, not out of happy affairs. Perhaps Burt was only using this mistress as an excuse to leave Gretchen. Perhaps he would not take up with her permanently.

The shopping cart was filled above the brim, and a loaf of bread slid from the top onto the floor. "Shit," said Nina, as she stooped to retrieve it. She parked the cart beside a pile of unopened cartons at the end of aisle six and went to get an empty one. After a vacation, it took two full carts to replenish her empty cupboards and refrigerator. As she headed for Dairy Products, Nina reflected that not many real people, leading real lives, genuinely want to be uprooted from their routines, their families, the blessed familiarity of their daily lives, by the realization of romantic fantasy, the materialization of the long-dreamed-of perfect one. She, for one, did not. She loved her husband and sons; her work days and holidays blended satisfactorily.

Nina went through the checkout procedure and, after writing her name and address on a card for the delivery boy, walked home. In the shabby lobby of her apartment building (few buildings spend significant money on lobbies these days) she stopped for the mail, which had been late, as it always is after a holiday. There were bills and one letter. It was from Nick Palladino. To David.

"Yup," she thought, "This is the kind of day where the only letter is from my first husband to my second husband."

Until now, when Nick wrote, he addressed both of them. What could he possibly have to say to David alone? Briefly she considered steaming open the envelope, but her integrity asserted itself, and she carried the missive upstairs and deposited it on the brass mail tray in the front hall. From the kitchen her called-out hello was echoed by Coral, the housekeeper. Walking down the long hall, she poked her head into the den, where Gregory and Zachary were watching television. Handsome boys, they were dark, like David.

"Hi, boys."

"Hi, Mom," they said in unison, their eyes fixed on the screen.

"Turn it off at five," she reminded them.

There was no answer. They were in third and second grades respectively at Twickham, and she took them to school in the morning, but Coral picked them up in the afternoon. Nina had found Coral through an employment agency. As a result of offering, from the start, a higher salary than the going rate, she had been sent only the best people. She had asked the boys to be present at the interviews and they had all agreed about Coral, an affectionate woman in her late fifties with grey hair and no waistline.

Nina often stayed after school for meetings or to work in her classroom and then, on the way home, did neighborhood errands, like going to the supermarket and picking up shoes from the shoemaker. She was confident that Coral would supervise the boys and give them hearty snacks when they returned from school, to tide them over, until seven-thirty family dinner. David was customarily home by seven o'clock, as he was on this evening.

He came into the living room and kissed Nina, who was curled up on their dark green sofa with *The New York Times,* which she rarely read before evening. The room was furnished with ethnic scatter rugs on polished parquet floors, clean-lined furniture, and reasonably indestructible cotton fabrics. Plants, books, records, and prints were arranged more for convenience than ambience.

"There was a letter for you," Nina observed dryly.

"From your ex."

"Did you read it?"

"Yes." He was teasing her.

She had to ask, "What'd he want?"

"His daughter by his first marriage . . ."

"Nicole."

"Nicole. Thinks she wants to become a lawyer. She'll be in New York, probably between Christmas and New Year's. He wants me to see her, give her the poop about practicing in Manhattan, show her my office—you know."

"Doesn't she want to practice in Los Angeles?"

"She grew up there. Thinks she may want to move here. She'll apply to Eastern law schools. He wants to be sure her visit here is at a time when it's convenient for me to see her."

"You could give her a recommendation."

"We'll see."

"Where will she be staying? Or haven't they planned in detail yet?"

"The Plaza. You may read the letter."

David went into the kitchen to fetch a Scotch and water for himself and a white wine and soda for his wife.

"Shouldn't we offer to put her up?" asked Nina when he returned.

"Who?" David sat down in his favorite dark-blue armchair, lit his pipe, and put on his glasses (which indicated that he intended to read).

"Nicole."

"Invite your first husband's first daughter by his first wife to be our houseguest? Today's extended family."

"Do you mind?" She approached David in gingerly fashion, because his greatest weakness was a nasty temper.

"Why should I?"

"That's a nondenial denial."

"If she doesn't object to the convertible sofa in the den and two small, obsessed television viewers spending several hours a day in her room, she's welcome. Personally, I'd prefer the Plaza."

"She'll probably be out a lot, but she might appreciate our companionship. And I'd like to spend some time with her. Is Christmas vacation okay with you?"

"Sure."

"She must be nineteen."

"Twenty."

Oddly, Nina was jealous. David and Nicole would go off to the office together or he would take her to lunch at a glamourous restaurant. She was not the child Nina remembered. Nick enclosed her photograph in his Christmas card every year, and the latest one revealed a tanned and leggy blonde.

"She looked very West Coast and spacey in the last photo," David commented.

"Yeah."

Nina pretended to read the paper, but she was examining the inside of her own head. Had Burt's defection made her insecure?

"Burt has left Gretchen," she announced.

David put down his section of the newspaper and waited for the story. She told him what had happened.

"Coward," was David's judgment on Burt. "Poor bastard. No guts."

"What about Gretchen?"

"Is she in bad shape?"

"She's amazingly cool. Their behavior mystifies me."

"She's had the long weekend to grieve."

"Subconsciously, you mean, she knew their marriage was kaput."

"How could she not?"

"They must have been thoroughly estranged already."

"That happens. How was the faculty meeting?"

"It went very well, really. I think we teachers feel a provisional optimism."

"You like Hinks?"

"Not exactly, but it's possible that he's the headmaster Twickham needs. He conducted the meeting with clarity and good humor. He's direct and self-assured without being arrogant."

"Can he handle that volatile crew? The faculty is a mass of rugged individualists."

"He seems to be a genuine leader—firm, intelligent. He's short. Shorter than I."

"You're five feet eight! Does he project that aggressive, bullying anger associated with shorter men?"

"Not at all."

"I hear reservations."

"He's going to change Twickham. What if I no longer fit in there?"

"You're flexible and he sounds reasonable."

"I suppose so." Nina stared, unfocusing, into the middle distance.

"Dad's home!" called a young voice from the arched doorway.

Gregory climbed onto the arm of David's chair to collect his hug and kiss. Zachary followed close behind, perching on the other arm. Until the housekeeper announced that dinner was served, the little boys held the spotlight.

# 2

※※※

# EVALUATION

On the first day of school, Nina's kindergarteners arrived with hovering mothers in hand, including the businesswomen, lending bona fide maternal support on this important occasion. After today, there would be a smattering of fathers, too, making drop-offs en route to their offices, and housekeepers, who would grow in number as school became for the children a routine, to carry them through childhood and adolescence and deposit them, willy-nilly, in the adult world. Every year it was the same, excitement and terror producing either bravura or clinging shyness in the tiny pupils.

Nina acknowledged that these precious, shining youngsters, fresh and vulnerable, would somehow metamorphose, over the decades, into the dim and prosaic people most grownups, in comparison, are. Her own days were filled with the care of human beings at their most beguiling, before they are restrained by life. She possessed a secret that few gleaned: no other teacher has as great an influence on the future as the kindergarten teacher; hers is true, raw power, because the tender psyches and minds under her tutelage are more malleable than they will ever again be.

On the third day of school, Mort Hinks appeared in the classroom doorway. Nina was writing the alphabet on the green chalkboard and calling on the children as they raised their hands to identify each letter.

"May I come in?" asked Mort, smiling.

Nina was expecting him. He had told the faculty that he hoped to visit every classroom during the first week, to meet the students. Being presented to them at an assembly, he felt, was too impersonal; small groups were more to his liking.

Nina pushed her tinted eyeglasses to the top of her head and beckoned him in.

"Children," she said, "this is Dr. Hinks. Dr. Hinks is the new headmaster of our school. You and he share something important. This is your first week at Twickham. Well, did you know that it's Dr. Hinks's first week, too?"

The children's faces reflected varying degrees of pleasure, bemusement, or indifference.

"That's right," said Mort, casting Nina a quick glance of appreciation for her cue. He sat on one of the low tables and faced the class, grouped in a patch of sunlight on the floor, in front of the chalkboard. "You and I are starting school together."

A few giggles.

"In fact, in a way, I'm newer than you are, because the school where I was headmaster before this is in another state, Massachusetts, and my family and I moved to New York during the summer. Imagine how exciting and strange it is for us. I'll tell you a secret. It's a little bit scary, too. Moving to a new apartment in a new town and going to a new school all at the same time!"

The children paid close attention. He was airing emotions they understood, and they wanted to see where he went with it. So did Nina.

"I'm a daddy," he continued, "but my two daughters are big girls. Gillian is sixteen, and she's a junior in the upper school.

Tessa is thirteen, and she's in the middle school. Even for big girls like them, going to a new school isn't easy. They worried about whether or not they'd make friends, whether the teachers would be nice to them, and what kind of schoolwork they'd be expected to do. Gillian, Tessa and I have all discovered that each day we get a little more accustomed to school, and now that we have an idea of what to expect, it's not nearly so scary. We do make friends, and the teachers at Twickham are very understanding. This is a terrific school, and we're proud to belong here. No one asks us to do anything that is really too hard for us. The more we relax, the more fun we have."

Nina listened intently. Several of the children smiled and nodded. This man spoke sense. Mort was wearing grey flannel slacks and a grey tweed sports jacket, with leather patches on the elbows. No tie. A button-down, white shirt, open at the collar, and his tortoise-framed glasses. Beneath his calculated casualness, Nina saw a purpose. "If we have a child at the age of six," the early Jesuits had said, "we have his mind for life." Nina inferred that Mort agreed with her: five is better, and Twickham was to be a benign and constructive force in children's lives—for the rest of their lives. That was a positive omen. No previous headmaster or headmistress had taken kindergarteners seriously enough to suit Nina. Mort's presence was, nonetheless, so forceful that it made her feel edgy.

"How many of you watch 'Sesame Street'?" Mort asked.

Every hand shot up. The 'Electric Company'? At least half of them viewed a program designed to teach remedial reading to older youngsters. Nina knew that Mort was interested in the influence of television on education. None of this was idle chatter. She suspected that he was playing to her, too, while he addressed the little ones, trying to gain her allegiance.

"Ms. Lathrop and I realize that you come to kindergarten already knowing many things about the world, and I imagine that one of the things you know quite a lot about is the alphabet. I noticed that you were studying that, when I came in. Will you say it for me?"

Her students looked uncertainly at Nina, who led the recitation, "A, B, C, D . . ."

When they had finished, Mort made some graceful parting remarks, and Nina walked him to the door. The corridor where they spoke smelled of floor wax and brass polish.

"How many students, when you first started teaching, already knew the alphabet?" he asked.

"Not nearly so many. They had it in nursery school, but they hadn't mastered it to the extent these kids have."

"Have you had to update your curriculum?" He stepped back from her.

"Some. They're still at the same level emotionally, but they acquire skills more readily, can do more, and are much more knowing than children I taught years ago."

"Thanks," said Mort. "See you this afternoon."

She had scored high, Nina thought, but this process of mutual assessment was not amusing.

Nina and the other kindergarten teacher, Peggy Vandercook, taught an afternoon as well as a morning group, since kindergarten lasted only a half day. In the other grades in the lower school, there were four teachers at each level.

Mort's afternoon appearance did not repeat the morning effort. The boarding school from which he had come excluded the youngest grades. He was trying not only to become a friendly and familiar figure for the children but to acquaint himself with who and where they were. He and Nina capitalized again on the newness that the headmaster and the kindergarteners had in common, but he skipped the alphabet and asked them about the city. This time Nina sat down next to him, in an attempt to feel more comfortable with him.

The children told about riding in busses, subways, taxis, and horse-drawn carriages (through Central Park). One boy, in an alligator shirt, said he and his family traveled to and from the airport in a limousine. They recommended the little zoo in Central Park and the big Bronx Zoo. A pigtailed girl raved about *The Nutcracker Suite* ballet at Christmas and the New York Philharmonic Orchestra's Young People's Concerts. The South Street Seaport Museum, the Empire State Building, and the Statue of Liberty were predictable favorites. As for art museums, the Junior Museum at the Metropolitan was popular for its objects to handle, buttons to push, light organ to play. The courtyard of the Modern was rated a great place to chase pigeons and throw pennies into pools, but a warning was issued never to climb on the sculptures, if there was a guard in sight. They complained about litterbugs.

Nina walked Mort to the door. He motioned her into the hall again. An overhead light had gone out and they were in shadow.

"What an amazing bunch. Are they all like this?"

"New York children are the most interesting kids I've ever known. That's why I'm here."

She sensed that her remark had alienated him and remembered that his own were not New York children; he probably found them and their friends fascinating.

"Of course there are terrific children everywhere," she added quickly, making it worse by communicating to him that she had understood his thoughts.

"Of course." He left her without trying to disguise the awk-
wardness of the moment, and she grudgingly gave him points for
that.


                              *


Mort soon announced the schedule for faculty meetings. He
was to meet with the teachers of the lower school in a large group
once a week, except during the last week of each month, when
they were to break up into smaller groups for more detailed
discussions. It was, Nina thought, like a college lecture group
dividing for seminars. Her seminar was set for Tuesdays and
would include the other kindergarten teacher and the four first-
grade teachers, as well as Mort and the music, art, shop and
physical education teachers.

Nina arrived at the faculty lounge for the first meeting in
October prepared to proselytize, determined to succeed now
where she had failed with the previous headmaster. The early
arrivals sat on couches and in armchairs. The rest used folding
metal chairs, which they took from a stack against the wall. As
usual, the air was stale with smoke, causing friction between
nicotine addicts and abstainers.

When the routine business of fire drills and assemblies was
out of the way, Nina plunged in: "We need a science teacher for
our kids."

The other teachers smiled and made a few here-she-goes-
again comments, but Nina was confident of their support, if she
could stimulate Mort's. She watched his face and saw the wash

of his responses: surprise, thoughtfulness, and doubt that there was a need.

"But you aren't familiar with the capacities and curiosity of the youngest kids," she replied, as if he had spoken. "They shouldn't have to wait until fourth grade to have science as a separate subject."

He considered, acknowledging her point silently, searching for a solution.

"You could sit in on our classes for an hour or so."

He digested her suggestion and accepted it. Before he had a chance to announce this decision, Nina turned to the other teachers and said, "We should all be dealing with science, for at least part of the time, while Mort's observing. I'll have started on the solar system."

Mort seemed to be delighted by her setting her five-year-olds to grapple with the universe, just for starters.

"Well, they love that," she said, smiling but defensive.

She glanced at Peggy Vandercook, the other kindergarten teacher (her contemporary and friend), beneath whose pose of polite attention Nina discerned perplexity. That the exchange between Nina and Mort was verbal only on her side but was as complete as if he, too, had spoken, seemed, while it was happening, natural to Nina. Peggy, however, found it unusual. Her knitting needles were motionless as she regarded them. Mort saw Nina seeing Peggy and smoothly covered, assuring the teachers that he would tell them in a couple of weeks which days he would observe their classes. Nina, like Peggy, said nothing for the rest of the meeting.

Nina walked home through Central Park from Twickham on the East Side to her West End Avenue apartment. It was one of those brisk autumn days that makes New Yorkers almost visibly bristle with excitement, optimism, and ambition. The trees, against the clear blue sky, seemed to refract sunlight in their reds, golds, and ambers; yet the grass was still green (thanks to an annoyingly rainy summer). She thought, " 'Pigeons on the grass, alas.' " And squirrels. And dogs, happily but illegally off their leashes. The earth smelled rich and fertile. Nina was suffused with the day.

She mused that there had been something opaque in her exchange with Mort at the faculty meeting. The man disturbed her. She found him overbearing. Still, she retained a sense of him even now: a flavor, a color, a smell—bleached beach grass, lemon verbena, yellow diamonds, and cheese soufflé. Nina shook her head vigorously, as if clearing water from her ears.

*

There are two subjects most kindergarteners particularly love: dinosaurs and our solar system. Why, year after year, this is so, Nina had not been able to interpret. She ordinarily taught dinosaurs during the first term and the solar system in the spring, because dinosaurs are easier. This year, determined to inspire Mort to convince the board of directors that a science teacher was imperative for kindergarten through third grade (there was currently one only for grades four and above), Nina crossed her fingers and handed out cardboard planets for her morning students to color.

Inasmuch as there are nine planets and one sun, six students were left wanting, so Nina gave each of them a piece of the asteroid belt, cut with irregular edges and fitting together like parts of a jigsaw puzzle. They formed a ring enclosing the sun and four inner planets when they were pushpinned to the strip of glossy black wrapping paper that dominated the bulletin board.

By the time Mort observed the younger classes, Nina's students were engrossed in their project. They had finished coloring their chunks of the universe and knew where they belonged in relation to each other. Before Mort arrived, Nina removed from the mural and gave back to the children the celestial bodies they had colored. Mort settled in the rear of the classroom.

"Who's first?" Nina began.

"Allison," cried the students.

"I am!" Allison took her thumb out of her mouth and waved her bright yellow sun.

"Come on," said Nina.

Allison proudly pinned the sun in the middle of the shiny black mural.

"Can you tell us something about the sun?"

"It's a star," said Allison.

"Very good. Who's next?"

One by one the diminutive scholars revealed that Mercury is the smallest planet, Venus the hottest, Earth the only one with intelligent living creatures; Mars has dust storms; Jupiter is the largest planet; Saturn has rings of ice, rock, and dust; Uranus has five moons (crayoned red, yellow, green, purple, and orange by the young artist who added it to the mural); Neptune is sometimes the most distant planet, but tiny Pluto usually is. Six facts about the asteroid belt were announced by the six children who had pieces of it.

Nina kept an eye on Mort. He was as impressed by the children's pleasure as by their knowledge and thanked them enthusiastically for sharing with him their solar system, asking if they would allow him to display it in the lobby. They were flattered but reluctant to part with their masterpiece, until Mort assured them that they could have it back.

Nina realized that during the upcoming parent conferences for the lower school, he wanted the mural to be seen by all parents, not solely those of her class. A crucial aspect of Mort's responsibilities was fund-raising, and schools were suffering financially, so every signal that proclaimed Twickham outstanding and worthy of donations must be flashed loud and clear. Nina's revulsion at using this heavenly project for crass commercialism was tempered: the money to pay the new science teacher had to be found. Furthermore, she ought to support Mort's efforts.

The afternoon session was also a success. Nina's other class pinned dinosaurs to a primitive landscape, provided by the art teacher, and related their outstanding characteristics. The exotic beasts were vividly real to the youngsters, and there was a short but lively discussion of what it would be like, if a dinosaur magically appeared in Central Park. Nina and Mort worked together well; their cogs meshed and the children loved the atmosphere they created.

As had happened several times before, Nina and Mort found themselves leaving school at the same time, late that afternoon. Since he lived on Central Park West, they walked through the park together. They always stuck to business, talking exclusively about school, almost never about themselves; occasional personal revelations slipped into their conversations. They were both wearing trench coats, and Nina hitched the strap of her tan bag up on her shoulder and shoved her hands into her pockets. The skyline was darkly beautiful against deepening blue; the air was crisp, suggesting frost.

"You're a fine science teacher," said Mort.

She looked sharply at him, narrowing her brown eyes.

Mort grinned. "It's true, you know. I don't see why we need a science teacher for the lower grades. If the other teachers are as skilled as you are, and I'll observe them all before I decide, I can't see why we do."

"Grade teachers can't do nearly enough. Buying the equipment for each individual classroom is out of the question, and anyway, we haven't the training to take these kids as far as they can go."

"An additional teacher is expensive. We have to cut back, not expand."

"I understand that. But for their generation, science is the single most important subject. It's not the place to cut back. I get tired of our being old fogies acting as if the last thirty years didn't change radically the future our students will have to cope with. I've seen first-graders playing computer games . . ."

Mort blanched.

"We can't afford a computer for the lower school yet, I know, but we should be budgeting for one, trying to raise money."

"Nina, in an ideal world, you'd get your science teacher. But inflation is hurting the entire educational system. We have to scramble to maintain our present standards."

"We have to keep getting better. It takes imagination and work."

"I *am* working. I'm being as imaginative as I know how. Short of having the art teachers set up a printing press in the basement, we can't afford another science teacher."

"You're still learning about Twickham," Nina flared. "Perhaps when you're on top of the job, you'll be able to find a way."

He was piqued by her condescension, but he admired her

conviction and passion. "I'm exceedingly well acquainted with the budget and its inadequacies. More so, I dare say, than you are."

She did not want to understand that he regretted turning her down. She wanted to be disappointed and furious, rather than, as she was, disappointed and sympathetic.

"Is that your final word?" she asked.

"I'm going to observe all the classes."

"But your mind is made up?"

"I hope my mind is never closed. There's not a hell of a lot I can do this year. Looking to the future, perhaps . . ."

"Tomorrow never comes," snapped Nina.

"You'd be surprised."

They walked the rest of the way in heavy silence.

After saying goodbye, Mort looked back at her, standing on the corner of Central Park West, waiting for the light to change. His eyes were sad, wry, and penetrating. She felt it in her gut: it was unalleviatedly a man-to-woman look, with none of the colleague disguising it. She stared at him, acknowledging it. The green "walk" light flashed, and they turned and strode away. Nina tried to quell the unexpected rush of feeling, the swelling of labia, by concentrating willfully on the street scenes around her. It did not really work. Damn him. She didn't even like the man.

# 3

## APPREHENSION

SITTING in her navy blue robe on the flagstone terrace, behind their converted barn in Connecticut, Nina sipped her coffee and beheld the morning. The mist had almost burned off the meadow, and it was golden in the sunlight. In surrounding trees, birds flitted and sang. Since it was nutting time, squirrels were at their busiest. The Lathrops' weekend retreat, although only two hours from Manhattan, was far enough north to be well along into autumn. Unlike the multihued trees in Central Park, these were almost bare, with only a few beige and russet leaves. Nina was glad that the evergreens presented a solid front of verdancy, regardless of seasonal changes. Samantha, the family's orange and white cat, stalked sleekly, her prey too small and well camouflaged to be spotted by Nina, who rooted for whatever-it-was and hoped that Sam would, uncharacteristically, fail as huntress.

Living in the country on weekends and during vacations made life in town possible. It was necessary, Nina and David found, to escape regularly, if they were to enjoy the pace and excitement of their city. How did Mort Hinks and his family stand it, confined to an apartment, after living on the campus of a country boarding school? Reflecting on the way Mort looked at

27

her after their most recent walk across the park, Nina slipped into a reverie.

It was alarming that she had responded with such obliterating emotion. Was there a lack in her life of which she was not conscious? She admitted that she had always thought that what she most wanted to share with a man was intimacy—emotional, intellectual, and sexual. Since she had not achieved it with either of her husbands, she had (quite recently) become reconciled to doing without intimacy. If she had the courage for such a risky encounter, would she not have married an equally adventurous man?

Nick, her first husband, was fiery and physical, making love with force if not finesse, screaming when he was angered, spending too much money on gifts when he was contrite, murmuring marvelously when he was tender. That had lasted for two and a half years. Nick was thirteen years her senior and she was twenty-five when they divorced. He remained her friend, still, taking an avuncular interest in her fortunes.

David came along and was bright and cool, compatible and reliable, a cultured lawyer exactly her own age, who was at the beginning of what was unmistakably going to be a respectable and lucrative career. Making the best decision of her life so far, she married him, when they were both twenty-seven. Now they were thirty-nine and their lives were intricately woven together into a warmly colored, oversized blanket, which wrapped around them both, keeping them snug, while leaving room to stretch and turn. What concerned Nina on this morning was a new awareness that she was more vulnerable to emotional surprise than she had realized.

After a family breakfast of oatmeal and toast, the boys began clamoring about Halloween, which was the following week.

"We'll pick our pumpkins today!" insisted Zachary.

"And we're going to carve them, too," added Gregory. "Will you help?"

Their parents exchanged glances, sharing the annoyance that they were not to have the morning free to themselves, while the boys played outdoors, but happy with the continuity a jack-o'-lantern brings to a family. These boys might regard walking on the moon as mundane, while for their parents it was amazing, but the ritual of carving a jack-o'-lantern was as exciting for them as it had been for their elders. David had helped them plant pumpkin seeds, which in turn had sent up a vine, which produced several pumpkins. After breakfast, the family trooped to the garden, David holding a small saw in one hand and Nina's hand in the other. After a discussion about the relative aesthetic merits of the orange gourds, Gregory and Zachary managed to choose different ones, rather than to pitch battle over the same one (as they had done the previous October). The boys took turns using the saw, severing their favorites from the vine. Nina, who had brought her camera, recorded the event.

"Are you going to draw the faces on first?" asked David, ever precise, as they walked back to the house.

"Naw, I know what I'm going to do," said Gregory. "I can see it in my mind."

"You might get it wrong," said Zachary, his father's son. "If you draw it, you can see what it looks like, before you cut. That way, you catch mistakes."

"I won't make a mistake."

"Everyone makes mistakes."

"Not me on a jack-o'-lantern."

"You're not so great."

"Okay, boys, knock it off," said David. Once such an altercation began, it might continue indefinitely, both sons wanting the last word.

The boys squatted in the grass outside the kitchen door, and Nina gave them sharp, sturdy knives and a large spoon for scraping. David, lighting his pipe methodically, sat down beside them to offer advice and prevent accidents.

"Mine's going to be weird," said Gregory. "I want it to be sort of freaky, Dad."

"Fine."

"I want a funny one," said Zachary.

Nina came out and handed a piece of charcoal to Zachary. "You can sketch on the face with this. You want a piece, Greg?"

"I said I didn't."

"Thanks, anyway," reminded David.

Eyes lowered. "Thanks, Mom."

"Shall we roast the seeds?"

"Sure!"

Nina laid down the pyrex bowl she had been carrying. Then she got a cookie sheet, covered it with aluminum foil, and wiped the foil with safflower oil. She set the oven at two hundred fifty degrees and, leaving the cookie sheet on top of the stove, picked up her camera and rejoined her family.

The pumpkins were hollowed out and the bowl was half-filled with seeds and damp, sticky, orange fibers. She snapped a picture of her three males and returned to the kitchen with the bowl.

"I cleaned off the seeds and salted them. They're in the oven," she announced a few minutes later.

"Thanks."

"Great."

The boys watched intently while David helped to carve the

face that Zachary had sketched. Its lopsided, toothy grin was as insouciant as their younger son and therefore reassuring. Gregory put aside his own work but resumed as soon as David and Zachary were finished. The boy backed off from his pumpkin, cocked his head on one side, and pondered. The asymmetrical, ominous face that resulted from his efforts would surely keep ghosts away as it burned in the window at night.

"We're going to ride our bikes," said Zachary when they had cleaned up.

"Be home for lunch by twelve-thirty," said Nina.

Gregory and Zachary coordinated their watches with the kitchen wall clock, a habit that they had learned saved them a lot of grief.

Nina and David headed for the woods. They loved to walk, dressed in jeans and lumberjackets, and to get caught up with one another's worlds. During the week, they were unravelled by the time the boys were in bed and they were alone together. Sitting now on their log by the brook, they watched the water and little fish and talked quietly, David puffing on his pipe. Nina felt close to him and very nearly content.

\*

One of Nina's students was stealing from others in class. Nina had talked to the parents and discovered that they were undergoing a vicious divorce and a custody battle over Dierdre, the troubled girl. It transpired that each parent wanted Nina to testify at the custody hearings: the mother, with whom Dierdre lived, asked Nina to swear that on Mondays, after she had been with her father for the weekend, her behavior was at a nadir; the father wanted Nina to testify that as soon as he moved out, at the end of September, Dierdre became a kleptomaniac. Nina was appalled, regarding both parents as too selfish to be fit. David, seeing the legal implications, warned her that before their divorce lawyers contacted her, she had better apprise Mort of the situation.

Mort's secretary was rearranging his bookshelves when Nina arrived in his office. Although Nina did not want Mort to think that she was maneuvering to be alone with him, which she preferred not to be, this was a matter to be discussed in private. She settled into a tan leather chair across the large desk from Mort, instead of on the dark brown leather couch under the window.

"I may be subpoenaed in a custody battle involving one of my students," she began.

There was an almost imperceptible twitch in the corner of Mort's left eye. "Beverly, why don't you leave those books for now? You probably have typing you'd like to get out of the way?"

Beverly turned and smiled at him, amused by his indirection. Her chestnut hair was pulled back and held with a ribbon, and her cheeks were rosy. She was six months pregnant and sanguine.

"Sure," she said, and she closed the door behind her.

"I've been approached by both of Dierdre Dobson's parents." Nina summarized the story, finishing with, "If Solomon told those two he'd cut the child in half, so they could each have a piece, they'd agree, rather than give an inch."

Mort was silent, waiting for his pain and ire to settle. He looked like a college professor, in his blue shirt and grey cashmere sweater; he was jacketless. Nina was also wearing a grey cashmere sweater.

Finally, Mort said, "We have two primary responsibilities. We want to do everything we can to help Dierdre, and we want to protect you from being drawn into the custody fight. If you become a decisive factor in this one—let's face it—a precedent will be set, which Twickham doesn't need any more than you do. Isn't your husband a lawyer?"

Mort tried to sound as if he knew the occupations of all faculty spouses, and Nina tried to look as if she believed that, but she was flattered.

"David says I'll have to give my opinion, if asked."

"What is your opinion?" He watched her carefully.

"I've thought a lot about it," she replied. "Legal custody doesn't mean much anymore, when disgruntled parents kidnap their children from ex-spouses, who have been granted legal custody, and get away with it by moving the kids out of state. The best solution for Dierdre, naturally, is for the parents to agree between themselves about custody, without slugging it out in front of a judge."

"The worst they know about each other will be on record, available to Dierdre, when she grows up."

"Oh, Dierdre! Her parents accuse each other publicly. Dierdre's friends' parents discuss it; some of my parents have approached me about the subject, but I refuse to open up. Their kids pick up bits and pieces and pass them back to Dierdre, who tries to pretend she doesn't care."

"But she's only five!"

Nina thought, "How did Mort get to be this old and preserve his empathy, keep his kindness intact, as keenly as he has?"

Her admiration must have shown in her face, because he lowered his eyes. "If it goes to court," he said, "what will your testimony be?"

"Dierdre's behavior has deteriorated steadily since school began. How could it not?" She looked away, too, at the large schefflera, which he had added in the corner of the headmaster's office, beside the couch.

"Is Dierdre worse on Mondays?"

Nina grimaced. "I can't see that she is."

"Was there a change for the worse at the end of September, when her father moved out?"

"I hadn't known her very long, but not that I observed. She was stealing right from the beginning of school, I just didn't know then who it was. She becomes more distraught week by week."

"Neither parent can gain anything if that's what you have to say." He was relieved.

"They're pressuring me to change. They phone me, ask to take me to lunch, to talk."

"You don't go?"

She frowned, wounded, and began fingering her brown curls.

"Thoughtless question," he acknowledged.

Nina moved forward to the edge of her seat. Being with this man was like being near a high tension line in the country; she felt the relentless vibrations.

"Mr. Dobson sent me, at home, four orchestra seats for *The Nutcracker*. I don't know how he knew I have two kids. I returned them." She smiled. "I was tempted to keep them and send him a check."

Mort was solemn. Nina sensed the wheels turning, the gears and levers and weights interacting in complex relationships, which awed her. Why had she felt hostile toward him until today?

"I'll ask the parents to come in and talk to me," he said.

"We can't twist their arms."

"We can apply moral pressure, and I'll remind them that although they're free to subpoena you, they're not to try to influence your judgment in any way. If you hold firm . . ."

"I shall."

". . . they won't want to call on you."

"They'd have nothing to gain."

"We're probably all right then."

He got up and passed her a wooden bowl full of red and yellow Delicious apples, which had decorated a side table. Looking into his face, so close to hers, the words sang in her head: "He's beautiful." She took a yellow apple and crunched into its sweetness. He left the bowl on his desk and, taking a red apple for himself, sat down again.

Nina said, "I want Dierdre to see Shirley."

Shirley Greene was the school's child psychologist.

"You've told the Dobsons?"

"Neither parent will give permission, because they're afraid, I surmise, that Dierdre will tell more about her home life than they care for anyone to hear from her."

Mort's face hardened. "What they're engaged in is child abuse. There are no bruises on the child . . . ?"

"No visible bruises. I've had the physical education teacher check."

"Has there ever been a Twickham student who was battered?" he asked, never having considered the possibility before.

"I remember one little boy whose parents were in *The Social Register.* When he changed for gym, there were cigarette burns on his back."

"My God!"

"We had to get involved. He went to live with an aunt and uncle, eventually, but it was harrowing for us all."

They were quiet, reflecting. Nina looked around the office and noticed that the paintings hanging on the wood-paneled walls were all signed by Catherine Myers, Mort's wife. They were good.

She wanted to say so but felt shy about discussing Kitty.

"Divorce needn't be so ugly." Mort's voice was flat.

"It's much harder on children than it's fashionable to admit."

"We have friends here who divorced when their daughter was in second grade and their son in fifth. The father lives in the East Eighties and the mother lives in the West Eighties. They walk back and forth with the children. They both have successful careers, and their secretaries check with each other before scheduling business trips, so one parent is always in town. The housekeeper, who takes care of the kids, lives where they do; she has a room at both the mother's and the father's."

Nina, looking into his blue eyes, which were especially bright because he wore a blue shirt, hoped that he had worn that becomingly blue shirt because he had an appointment with her.

To him, she said, "Life is better for children whose natural parents stay married and make loving homes for them."

"If parents remarry, the kids may discover that living with a man and woman who genuinely, deeply love each other, is happier and provides better role models than living with parents who are faking it or making do, for their sakes."

Nina thought, "Are Kitty and he faking it? Going through the motions? Kitty, who may have ironed that blue shirt? But Kitty can't iron. She sent it to the laundry and hung it in his closet when it came back. Wrong again, he can't afford to have his shirts returned on hangers, like David's; they probably come back folded around a cardboard, and Kitty puts them in his dresser drawer."

She said, "How many second—or third—marriages are that happy, are genuinely loving enough to make up to the children for not living with both natural parents?"

He stared at her calmly, riding out the surge of inappropriate feelings she suddenly aroused in him.

"Children are strong," she continued, disconcerted and excited. "But parents today take advantage of that."

She looked around for somewhere to deposit her apple core. He indicated a clean ashtray.

"You're unequivocally against divorce!" His eyes twinkled. "Sweet old-fashioned girl. Sorry. Sweet old-fashioned person."

She blushed. "I wish I were able to be. Most people do the best they can. At school, we pick up the pieces. We've discussed it, the staff has, and we've seen divorce come as a benefit to children from tense, angry homes."

She was fingering her short curls again. Mort refused to speak, although his concentration on her was absolute, so she blurted, "Sometimes, if it's handled sensitively by parents who've fallen in love with other people, it works out well." Her blush deepened.

"Maybe more mature parents manage it better," he suggested, his voice trembling slightly.

"New York parents tend to be older than average." She stared at him helplessly, then forced herself to continue with composure. "Most of my parents are in their thirties, even forties. Because many of the women have careers, their babies come late, and I find these older parents often produce the most interesting children, because of their own breadth of experience." She was fiddling with her gold chain necklace, frightened by the compelling attraction she was feeling for this man. The room became brighter, the objects in it had a new solidity and definition in his presence.

Mort accepted his emotions for her, monitoring them, watching her, without making demands or excuses. He was neither impelled to do anything nor compelled to avoid it. He was waiting for whatever evolved.

"Shall I speak to the Dobsons about letting Dierdre see the psychologist?" he asked, when he was satisfied that they had read one another correctly.

"That won't do any good." Her voice was nearly inaudible.

His feelings were hurt. "I can make it impossible for them to refuse."

Her face lit up with a transparent smile. "I'm sure you can!" She got up quickly and moved toward the door.

As she reached it and held out her hand to the knob, Mort was behind her, trying to open the door for her. Their hands brushed and she jerked hers back so violently that the gesture had the force of a confession. Watching his face, as the confirmation of her desire sank in, was like watching while an object, which one had inadvertently dropped into a deep, still lake, descended slowly, surely, through perfectly clear water—mesmerizing and beyond retrieval. Mort opened the door and Nina fled.

"I can't believe this is happening," she kept repeating to herself. "I hardly know the man. Nothing David could criticize has happened, yet I feel guilty. I can't be certain that Mort feels the way I'm certain he feels. I hope we don't because we mustn't."

\*

During the next few days, Nina arranged her routes through the school halls and her lunch hour so that she avoided Mort entirely. On the following Tuesday, there was a faculty meeting for the kindergarten and first grade teachers, and since it was a small group, she had to look at Mort and converse with him. She wore the most unbecoming combination of clothes she could devise and did not wash her hair that morning, although it needed it: not that she looked seedy, but she did look her worst. She was determined to defantasize herself and Mort, having convinced herself that was the solution (if there were, in truth, a problem).

As she entered the faculty lounge, Mort looked at her absently, did a double take, and comprehended her intention. It affected him more sharply than her prettiest outfit could possibly have done. His expression said, "Is it really that bad?" and then became an admission that it was.

"Oh hell!" she thought, sinking into one of the black vinyl armchairs. "How am I supposed to resist being understood?"

Peggy Vandercook brought Nina a cup of coffee, breaking the trance into which she had all too obviously sunk. Nina thanked her and pulled from her purse a list of notes on topics she wanted to discuss. She became businesslike. Mort behaved almost naturally. Immediately after they had adjourned, Nina left school, hoping to avoid meeting him. They reached the front steps simultaneously but quickly suppressed their dismay with polite, pointedly casual greetings. Nina paused to tie a green paisley scarf over her brown curls.

"Damned if I didn't forget something," Mort said awkwardly, as he retreated into the building.

Nina floated home, convinced that he was as drawn to her as she was to him, and incapable of regretting it. Her courtships had been relatively unobstructed, with the men as ready to meet her as she was to meet them. This was different. She wanted Mort and she could not have him. Ever. Yet she did not believe the impossibility.

"My emotions are completely out of control," she said aloud.

A boy on a bike passed and gave her a strange look. She wished bikers would stay off the sidewalks.

Mort was not tall nor dark nor handsome, not the sort of man who had ever interested her, but she found herself free-associating that he was small of stature and that *petit mort* is a French idiom for an orgasm. Men were cruising her, more than they had in years, more than when she was in her twenties. She knew why. She exuded elation and desire. Nina recognized that she had to treat the situation, covert as it was, seriously.

Being a list maker, when she reached home she sat down at the pine desk in the dining room, placed there because the den was given over to television, bookshelves, and a convertible sofa for guests. On a yellow legal pad she wrote with a blue felt-tipped pen the real reasons that she and Mort should not merge, however fleetingly, for (she imagined) if they started, they might not be able to stop:

*1. We're both happily married.* Well, if not blatantly happy, at least contented. Surely Mort and Kitty had as satisfactory a marriage as hers with David. Nina had met Kitty Hinks at a couple of school functions. Kitty, an artist, painted under her maiden name, Catherine Myers, and sold her paintings through a gallery where she'd been showing for years. Blonde hair worn parted in the middle, shoulder length and straight; petite; soft voice; socially gracious and adept; a class act. Obviously she had been gently raised by a family with good blood lines and no recent familiarity with serious economic insecurity. The kind of person that Nina had grown up wishing she were.

*2. Our children deserve to live with both their natural parents.*

She and, she inferred, Mort, believed with an old-fashioned fervor that the family should be protected and preserved. You choose to have children (they do not choose to have you), and the implied contract is that their well-being is your responsibility. Where that means postponing your own personal growth and cramping your life style, so be it. You had your chance before they were born, and then you produced them, and now it is their turn; you'll have a turn, again, after they are fledged. Natural parents are obliged to get along well enough to provide a nurturing family circle, because that's best for youngsters. Nina had little patience with the frivolous attitude toward marriage and parenting, which so many of her contemporaries mouthed to the media, favoring their own interests over the interests of their dependent children. Gregory and Zachary pledged her to try valiantly to stick with David. Who knew where a love affair might lead?

*3. I love my job and Twickham.* If she and Mort became an item, she would become unemployed. How liberal can a liberal school board be expected to be? Headmaster outranks kindergarten teacher, regardless of seniority. If only one of them were kept on, it would not be she.

*4. Mort loves his job and is proud of Twickham.* It was, of course, possible that the consummation of their relationship could lead to the nullification of his contract. How liberal can a liberal school board be expected to be? This was the best and biggest job of Mort's career and required his best and biggest effort, unadulterated by moonings and yearnings for the excitingly new, fascinatingly different, confoundingly compatible mind and body of an erotically aroused senior staff member.

*5. My life works, and I don't want to risk it.* Time and effort had produced a balance in her roles as wife-mother-teacher and city dweller–country-house co-owner, which, now that she had achieved it, she wished to enjoy.

6. *Mort and I don't know each other very well, except intuitively.* Propinquity might prove devastating or, worse, boring.

7. *Money.* A headmaster's earnings never approach those of a partner in a law firm as prestigious as Burgess, Lathrop and Hoffman. Recently David had won his first megaclient, a communications conglomerate, and he was going to be genuinely rich. If she lived with Mort, he would be paying child support and alimony; her salary would go toward household expenses rather than remaining her private cache to spend as she chose. Who knew where a love affair might lead?

8. *I am the captain of my fate.* She was not passion's plaything. She could subdue her feelings and control her actions. She would avoid Mort as much as possible and be casual, perhaps indifferent, when they met.

Nina folded up her list and put it under the false bottom in her jewelry box, where she could get at it, if she needed inspiration. She resolved to change the way she thought about Mort: she was blessed to work with a man who cared about her as he apparently did and to return his concern; they need not categorize their emotions, merely accept them. It is all right to care (to love?) so long as one's behavior is prudent and one's eyes do not send intimate messages.

# 4

✕◇✕◇✕

## REFLECTION

THE Lathrops had decided to stay in town for Thanksgiving, this
once, to permit the boys to see the Macy's Parade live (rather
than, as in previous years, on television in the country). When
David came home early on Wednesday, Coral was filling the
refrigerator with dishes ready to be cooked the next morning.
Nina sat at the desk in the dining room, bent upon reconciling
her checkbook with the latest bank statement. She succeeded as
David walked in the front door, so they met in the living room.

David lit his pipe and they briefly exchanged highlights of
their days.

"Did your checkbook balance?" He removed his impeccable
tie.

"After several attempts."

"Your savings account is fat?"

"Fairly."

"You won't spend your own money for clothes, so I'd like
to make a donation."

Not this discussion. Ever since his firm had acquired their
big, new client, he had been hounding her to improve her ward-
robe.

"My clothes are okay."

"Okay is not okay. As soon as the holidays are over, we'll be involved in dinners with my clients. You have nothing to wear."

"I do so."

"Nothing smart."

"Lay off, David."

"When are you going to grow up? Names are not destiny."

Nina was sensitive about her name meaning, "little girl," in Spanish. She had worked hard for whatever maturity she had developed, but she could hardly change her name to *Mujer,* "woman."

"I *am* grown up."

"That's open to debate."

"You lawyers!"

"You *married* me."

Nina was too surprised to reply, but he was not finished with her.

"I see Coral is preparing the Thanksgiving feast," he said. "What kind of stuffing are we having?"

"Sausage."

"Not again!"

"We all like it."

"What brings you to that conclusion?" He was icy.

Nina fumbled. "Uh . . . well . . ."

"Because I eat it docilely year after year?"

She smiled ironically. "Guess that must be it."

*"It's not funny."* He was livid.

Nina tried simultaneously to deal with him and to figure out what had set him off.

"Would you like to choose the stuffing for the Christmas turkey?" she asked.

"I'm not one of your fucking students."

"They have more self-control."

"I *pay* for sausage stuffing but I hate it. Disgusting. This household is run for the boys and you and supported by me."

"If I'd known you didn't really like . . ."

"You'd know if you cared. Henceforth, instruct your marvelous Coral to ask *me* before she indulges in one of her cooking orgies. We have too much food, anyway. Most of the world's peoples are starving to death. Our holiday meals are obscene."

"You're raving."

"I must be, to put up with you."

She glared at him.

"You ask *me,* before you make any plans for this family."

"Do you think we ought to switch to scented toilet tissue?" she inquired sarcastically.

"With the shit that goes on in this household, it might not be a bad idea." He stood up.

Nina heard him yelp at the boys in the den, where they were playing, evicting them so he could watch television alone. They came to her for comfort.

"What's wrong with Dad?" asked Gregory, his brown eyes anxious.

"He didn't say hello," said Zachary.

He pushed his straight, dark hair out of his eyes, and Nina realized that she had to remind Coral to take the boys to the barber.

"I don't know," she replied semitruthfully. "He must have had a bad time at the office. You go play in your room."

Nina sat quietly. David's flare-up had not been about stuffing or clothes. David had, she suspected, been picking up her uneasiness recently, had felt (without knowing why) that she was slipping away from him. She recalled the touch of Mort's hand on

hers, that day in his office. It was the only time that their flesh
had met. Mort's skin was different from any other she had known:
had she perceived an electrical force radiating from the surface
or was his skin denser? She was unable to name the sensation,
which was seductive and repellent, not disgusting, but too power-
ful.

Nina had noticed that she could listen to a love song on the
radio or watch a beautiful sunset without a twinge. The hearts-
and-flowers romantic spell that had made her dreamy in her youth
was no part of her current experience. Whatever it was she shared
with Mort, it did not depend upon props. They had done that
separately in their salad days, and now they wanted to share an
entrée.

There would be relief in not confronting one another. Most
of Nina's emotional energy of late had been expended in resisting
her longing for Mort, while watching him resist his longing for
her. Their struggle did not grow easier, as they had expected, and
she was bewildered and exhausted. Poor David. He deserved her
loyalty. Nina would use the four-day holiday ahead to concentrate
on him and to try to banish Mort from her thoughts.

*

The Lathrop family went to the Macy's Parade while Coral
prepared dinner. Nina had revised the menu and surprised David
with oyster dressing (this had meant a last-minute dash to the
local fish market). The boys said it was revolting and had double
helpings of mashed potatoes to compensate. David ate three

servings of dressing, pleasing Coral as much as Nina. In the afternoon, David watched football on television, and Nina took the boys ice skating, while Coral, jewel of jewels, cleaned up.

David's office was closed on Friday, too, and he and Nina left the boys at home with Coral and had a lingering lunch at a favorite Italian restaurant, where one could watch pasta being made from scratch. They strolled along Fifty-seventh Street and up Madison Avenue.

"Kitty Hinks has a one-woman show here," said Nina, in front of an art gallery, suddenly remembering.

"I don't see her name."

"Catherine Myers. She paints under her maiden name."

"Let's have a look." David pulled his glasses out of a pocket and put them on.

They climbed a stairway to the second-floor exhibit. Several people were moving slowly around the room, pausing thoughtfully before the canvasses. Kitty's work was representational, but she reduced landscapes, plants, objects, and people to geometric forms in bright, clear pastels. The men and women who had come to see them were familiar types and as engaging, Nina found, as the works of art. Their intelligence and individuality were stated in their faces, their clothes, the way they related to one another and to the paintings. She had seen them in many other galleries over the years. They were one of the myriad reasons she loved New York.

Nina recognized that she was avoiding Kitty's works, glancing at them and then at the people. She concentrated. Trying to imagine herself the artist, she strained to know how it felt to be Kitty. Kitty, it seemed, was a person whose inner world was more vibrant and highly developed than Nina's. How much time and space did that leave for Mort? Would the real woman please stand

up: Catherine Myers or Kitty Hinks? Nina's fantasies were not
nearly as available as Catherine's. Having an assertive inner vision
must be satisfying in ways Nina almost envied. All this, and Mort
too.

"Wow!" said David, as they descended the steep stairs.

"Really?"

"Don't you think she's amazingly good? I'd never heard of
her before this year."

"I'd heard of her, and Mort has her paintings in his office."

"To think that little princess is harboring a large talent."

Nina did not like the "princess" any better than she liked
the "large." She could accept gracefully Mort's wife's being talented, but not too talented. David had never intimated that she
had a "large" talent as a kindergarten teacher. He was proud of
her, but he was not impressed. Kitty, apparently, impressed him.

As they continued up Madison Avenue, Nina wondered how
important Kitty's talent was to Mort. Did he see her work as a
confirmation of her worth and superiority or as a rival for her
attention? Did he love her because she painted or in spite of it?
Her current show had been favorably mentioned in the *Times*.
The *Times* never reviews teaching performances. Strangers never
came to appraise, perhaps admire, her contribution to society.
Nina felt diminished. Depressed. A man cannot take seriously a
woman who devotes her career to five-year-olds, when he has
espoused a woman with original insight and the skill to express
it. Can he? Mort's job indicated that he valued education, but
Kitty's pursuits supplied a foil for his own. And now David was
becoming a Catherine Myers fan. Terrific.

At home, Gregory and Zachary bounced into the front hall
as their parents were hanging up their coats.

"Come and see what we built!"

"Mom! Dad! Come into our room."

In their doorway, David surveyed the clutter of toys and games used and then left where they lay, the records without jackets, the books piled on the carpet, and remarked, "Your room should be closed by the Board of Health."

"Tomorrow is picking-up day," Nina decreed.

The boys were too intent on showing off their accomplishments to listen. Nina and David stood over them as they explained how the red, white, and blue Lego rockets were ready to blast off.

"Those rockets are elegant," said Nina. "Who put them together?"

"We both did. These are mine."

"These are mine."

"I've always said you have a good sense of design. Is this the launch pad?" David pointed to a Lego construction.

"We made that together."

The brothers pointed out the space station that had been built with wooden blocks. They had drawn computers on the walls of the control room.

"It's wonderful," their parents agreed.

"Can we have some Ovaltine?" asked Zachary.

"Mixed in the blender?" added Gregory.

"Help yourselves," said Nina.

"Bring me a glass, would you?" said David. "I'll be in the living room."

"Captain Midnight lives," murmured Nina, heading for a fragrant tub, antidote to the blues. Her sons had cheered her up a bit, but she was still feeling low. Steeping in hot water, she imagined inviting Mort and Kitty to dinner. She and David gave lively dinner parties. They would ask two other couples, eight in all. In fantasy, the evening uncoiled. While she and David played happily married host and hostess (typecasting, more or less), Mort and Kitty displayed their coupleness and engaged the others in interesting *tête-à-têtes*. Nina and Mort, meanwhile, spied on one another's marriages. In an extremity of masochism, Nina saw herself make friends with Kitty, placing Mort beyond the pale. She had actually spoken to Kitty at faculty gatherings and sensed an effortless rapport with her, also. Being incapable of carrying on with a friend's man, Nina might thus permanently bury the potential for . . . what? If she and Mort ceased all resistance and gave in (which, of course, was not going to happen), what then? She chose not to conjecture. She also chose not to give that particular dinner party.

Nina donned a long challis dress, her favorite for cozy evenings at home, and (on an impulse) retrieved her old diary from a box, stored on the top shelf of a hall closet. She sat on the patchwork quilt that covered her king-size bed, a cup of tea with honey on the captain's chest beside her, and searched until she located the period covering the summer before she entered college. She read the entry reflectively, her face contorting with embarrassment and tenderness for that long-ago girl. Nina was able to feel once again the yearning and optimism of her lost self. The diary had lain unread for two decades, and it bridged those years as effectively as a science fiction time machine. Nina stood at both ends of more than twenty years of her life, the passionate expectations of the eighteen-year-old overlapping the seasoned recollections of the thirty-nine-year-old, forming a double image. The disparity was searing.

The dozen years ahead, she had believed at that point, were to be the most exciting of her life. From thirty on, life became vague, but she had supposed one built upon what one had. She had already known that, after graduate school, she was to become a teacher. All that had come to pass as forecast, with few major shocks of either disillusionment or gratification. Adjustments had been made. A school administration can be as maddening as any other. There was paper work that rankled, meetings that wasted time. The familiar frustrations of functioning in what passes for the adult world had been endured.

The other essential component in her wishful prophesy had been finding and keeping a man. At eighteen, that man was hidden in romantic mists but (mortifying to admit) his charisma was to be absolute: a knight in shining armour, Prince Charming with a beautiful kingdom to share, Heathcliff, Robert Jordan (yes, she expected the earth to move). Hopeless. How could her girlhood dreams have been woven of such ridiculous clichés and idealizations? She had not been naive in other ways. Nina was as still and quiet as a birdwatcher, while the ghosts of those dreams and longings flitted by. She paid close attention to that girl. Embarrassment left her but tenderness remained. Nothing wrong with those dreams. They were, essentially, honorable. Primitive, maybe. Silly in their symbolism. But wanting to connect intimately with a man was all right. Better than being so narcissistic that you needed, at heart, to be in a crowd.

The more Nina had lived, the less she had dreamed. She married Nick, divorced him, tried again with David. The marriages had provided sufficient satisfactions to distract her from the truth about how far they were from what she had once wanted. Nina closed her diary, but she did not return it to storage; she slipped it into a drawer of her early-American dresser, underneath her flannel nightgowns. She thought, "I'm becoming a squirrel, with my diary hidden in my lingerie and my list of reasons that Mort and I mustn't get together in my jewelry box."

She sat back against the ruffled pillows and finished her tea. Her students, presented with a collection of found objects, each chose a different assortment and constructed an individual collage; from the materials of her life, Nina made choices and made do, constructing an amiable life, if not an exuberant one. Accommodating. A good sport.

Two sentences from *The New York Times Book Review* applied, she feared, to her marriage. Anatole Broyard wrote: "While such a relationship lacks the romantic extravagance that so many of us hope for in the unreasonable depths of our hearts, it succeeds for perhaps the same reason. Its demands can be comfortably met." In her earlier youth (she considered herself still young, not middle-aged, though realizing that technically she was the latter), Nina had always truncated her most passionate romances before they became "too serious." The men had a way of being inappropriate for more than a fling. These days she was tougher and hungrier. Time nudged. She itched to risk and to win.

# 5

## ACKNOWLEDGMENT

NINA and Peggy Vandercook took their kindergartener's to the Museum of Natural History each year to see the giant Christmas tree, with its bright origami ornaments. The art teacher, Linda Babcock, attended their planning meeting in Mort's office. Her red hair was twisted into a knot on top of her head, giving her an old-fashioned air, which she cultivated by wearing white, frilled blouses. She explained how inspired the children were, seeing the tree and its golden brontosauri, tigers folded from striped wrapping paper, jellyfish with tinsel tentacles, shining birds and bats fluttering from mobiles—countless creatures inviting delighted recognition. The next day, in art class, when Linda passed out squares of colored paper, the children were receptive.

"It's a cinch to get them to watch my origami demonstration," she concluded.

"You make origami Christmas tree ornaments?" asked Mort, who had swiveled his desk chair to face the women sitting on his long, leather couch.

"They're birds, beasts, and fish, with thread-loop hangers."

"Everyone makes clay Menorahs for Hanukkah, too," said Nina, cool and distant.

"We have a top notch art program," Mort replied, looking at her impersonally, then smiling at Linda.

"About our field trip," said Peggy, holding on absently to a leaf of the schefflera plant next to her (she had forgotten her knitting). "We'll take our morning classes to the planetarium, adjacent to the museum."

"The afternoon classes will visit the dinosaurs," added Nina. "On a different day."

"We take them in chartered vans, since a bus is too large for only two classes." Peggy surreptitiously reached under her sweater and unbuttoned her tattersall skirt; she had put on weight over the holiday.

Mort looked from Peggy to Nina without evident preference. Peggy went along with the gag. She had been following (with a secretiveness that matched theirs) Nina's and Mort's struggle. She had never married and lived with a woman friend, who looked amazingly like her: boyishly cut brown hair, plump body, large breasts, and small facial features.

Nina and Mort projected indifference, having used the four-day break to repair their fences. Nina's inner softening had, paradoxically, strengthened her self-control. By the end of the meeting, Nina wondered if Mort were attracted to her at all. If he had detached himself from her, and if that were what she wanted, then why was she panic-stricken? Had she imagined their enthrallment?

For several weeks, Nina and Mort maintained their facades of normalcy, sharing a numbness that neither trusted. Nina did not see herself as a *femme fatale* or as a homewrecker (of one home, much less two). She had never been excessively alluring to men, but she liked and got along well with them. It was that alone, in fact, that alienated her from leading feminists: their self-portraits as victims of men seemed grotesque. It was not until later that Nina finally read a feminist novel that convinced her that a woman may live all her life without knowing a good man. Nina came to understand that this is true, but it was so far from her own autobiography that those sisters remained as foreign as fish; she did not know if they were superior to the men who surrounded them, as they claimed to be, but she questioned it.

A welcome aspect of the latent period in Nina's and Mort's adventure was the cessation of physical desire. Nina was not, she kept telling herself, a sex maniac, but Mort aroused in her inordinate lust. His image even flashed in her head when she was making love with David. She and David had an unremarkable sex life, with frenetic activity as infrequent as sustained abstinence. This did not prevent her from wanting Mort, and when the wanting stopped, she was relieved. A small voice reminded her that people who leave shelter during the eye of a hurricane soon face certain buffeting. She was, however, modest about her own magnetism and was not convinced that she represented a clear and present danger to the accomplished husband of a pretty, gracious, and talented artist.

As Nina's menstrual period approached, her irritability increased and her patience decreased. She was adept at disguising her discomfort in school, but with her family she was short-tempered. At the peak of her bitchiness, she and Mort found themselves walking home together for the first time in weeks. It was cold and Nina pulled up the hood of her raccoon coat. Hoods, she thought, are romantic. The day was darkening, and they stuck to the Seventy-second Street transverse through Central Park, rather than taking a more isolated route. So unprepared were they to be together that they were speechless. Their silence implied intimacy. Their defensive accretions dropped off. They were in a state of instar.

Nina heard her own waspish voice break the spell. "We ought to have more assemblies in the lower school."

Mort merely raised his eyebrows. She watched his face by the light from passing cars and from streetlamps.

Whiny: "My kids feel so tiny and at the bottom of the heap."

Evenly: "They're robust and cheerful whenever I visit your classroom."

"They're keenly aware of the pecking order." What was she doing?

"And assemblies?" He was resolutely nonargumentative.

"They'd feel like a more organic part of the school, attending assemblies with the older children on a regular basis." She was powerless to stop.

"Suggest that at a faculty meeting." His composure exacerbated her tension.

High and angry: "Will you support me?"

Heavy silence. That was it. They both heard it. The anxiety that had been building in her during these days of withdrawal. There was a catch in Mort's stride, but they kept up the pace, oblivious to traffic, to the cold seeping into their toes and fingers. Nina was humiliated by having confronted him. She was afraid she was going to cry.

Mort kept looking straight ahead. His arm brushed hers, and then he was holding her gloved hand in his: holding her hand, no mistake about it. There is nothing remarkable about a forty-five-year-old man and a thirty-nine-year-old woman walking hand-in-hand through Central Park. For this particular pair, however, a long-submerged capacity for ardor surfaced with ferocity fed by years of loneliness. Nina was in such blissful confusion that only later did she reflect upon the chance that they had taken. What if they were recognized by a friend, colleague, parent, student—mate? Someone hidden within a private automobile or a taxicab, unseen and threatening? Nina was unable to worry. She was warm and safe. While they strolled, gloved hand in gloved hand, neither spoke. Perhaps neither of them could speak. When they parted wordlessly, their eyes did not meet. Mort squeezed her hand and left her standing on Central Park West. Nina was convinced that if she really concentrated, she might levitate. Totally inappropriate, under the circumstances. How can holding hands be thrilling for a woman who has borne two children? Her face was luminous.

Nothing had changed at home. Naturally. Coral, in the kitchen, did not scowl disapproval at her. The boys, at their desks doing homework, did not reject her. Nina was free to flop on the patchwork quilt covering her bed and relive their park walk. Tears silently moistened her cheeks; that was a first. She had cried in despair over men but never before from intimacy's fulfillment. She had begun their walk feeling angry at Mort, but now she understood that she had no cause for anger. He was unfailingly reliable and honorable toward her and maintained his lovely dignity without hiding behind it. Her rage at him had been displaced.

In a white-out on the mountains, the landscape disappears; Nina's familiar interior scenery was effaced by her comprehension of Mort's innocence, in relation to her. A Seattle friend had told her that climbers to the summit of snowy Mount Ranier fry eggs over the steam escaping from cracks in that dormant volcano. Nina gazed at the fissure in the crust where her fury fizzed forth. Where was the hidden source? Was the supply of hoary wrath inexhaustible? With Mort, she moved hand in hand into the calming, balmy piney woods, with their heart-lifting verticals, filtered pure light, and soul-centering scent. She and he could immerse themselves in clear lake water, which would buoy and heal them. Being admired and loved by a blameless and beautiful man (as she surely was) conferred permission to divest herself of anachronistic grudges and the ancient habit of surrogate retaliatory strikes. All this from merely holding hands? That was the culmination. Nina was lulled into a dreamy half-sleep. She was awakened by David's kiss on her forehead.

"It's almost time for dinner," he said, drawing on his pipe.

She stretched and got up, giving him a friendly kiss in passing. At dinner, she listened intently to David's anecdotes, made the inane puns that elicit laughter from seven- and eight-year-olds, and was as gay as she was happy. She was amazed and disconcerted by how easy it was. If David perceived that, especially for this time of the month, her behavior was uncharacteristic, he kept it to himself.

\*

There were only a few more days of school before Christmas vacation. Whenever she thought she might meet Mort, Nina's muscles became taut, her speech rapid, and her face unnaturally warm. The day after their walk, he stopped her in the hall. Children's Christmas and Hanukkah drawings lined the walls. In Nina's favorite, Santa's reindeer wove around the lit candles of a Menorah. Mort asked about Dierdre Dobson.

"She's seeing a shrink," replied Nina. "Her parents let her

see our psychologist, as they promised you, but they asked Shirley to recommend a private therapist. Dierdre goes twice a week, after school."

"Has she stopped stealing?"

"Yes, but her behavior is erratic. The best news is that her parents are dropping the custody dispute. They're going to try joint custody: fifty-fifty. I think the therapist shamed them into that. I hope it works and Dierdre is helped. Repressing strong feelings can be very self-destructive."

Nina blinked swiftly several times. She had meant to avoid *double entendre.*

Mort's smile flickered and was extinguished, but its warmth lingered in his eyes. Although there were others passing in the hall, he took her right hand in both of his and held it, saying, "The best card dealt to Dierdre is you."

He let her hand drop and walked away. The gesture had not been compromising, but it was, she thought, brave. Nina continued to her classroom, shaking her head and making little "hmph" noises under her breath. Fantasies do not come true, not ever, not hers. Yet Mort's behavior did not deny what had happened; nor did it hint at apprehension.

In the remaining days, he neither withdrew nor drew closer. When they met, he was relaxed and as caring as the situation permitted. He was marking time. Nina, believing (as she had been raised to believe) that the man is the initiator, was agitated, never sure that he would not either make an overt gesture or disappear behind coldly correct formalities. While she acknowledged, with the feminists, that a woman ought to feel free to ask a man to dinner or to join her for a movie, this new liberty did not, in her lexicon, extend to the privilege of inviting a man to commit double adultery: that ought to be his idea. Nina pondered her position as she walked home alone during a snow flurry. White flakes thickened her lashes and wet her cheeks; she stuck out her tongue to catch their tiny pricks of cold.

"What the hell are you doing?" she asked herself silently. "If you're willing to be led down the primrose path, and I suppose you are, you should be willing to head the excursion, too."

"But," she inwardly answered herself, "that wouldn't be any fun."

"Aha!" she exclaimed. "You see. It's the same old knot. You are aroused by male aggression, you wallow voluptuously in your own passivity, you want to be overcome. Your most exciting fantasies have always, since your daydreams about being stranded on a deserted tropical island with your ninth-grade English teacher, involved being overwhelmed, against your will, by physical power, by threats, or best of all, by mutual passion."

"This is different," she protested weakly.

"Different!" her feminist sympathizer snorted. "Oh sure, sure. Being overcome implies *shame*, because you're *not responsible*, and shame is *sexy*. It's allied to what Norman Mailer is supposed to have said: women now in their twenties don't attract him because they don't know sex is dirty."

"Sex isn't dirty."

"Don't intellectualize. Your fantasies of succumbing to force are dirty and have the same source as your desire to have an affair with Mort. You think overweening passion relieves you of all responsibility to David and Kitty, to Gregory, Zachary, Gillian, and Tessa. The shame of it! How exciting! How sexy!"

"Shut up," Nina replied sullenly. "Sex with Mort can't be dirty."

"Right. But getting there is dirty, or 'illicit' if you prefer, and is all the more titillating for that. You being so helpless and all."

"Woody Allen says sex is dirty, if it's done right. Anyway, I can't help it."

"Mmmm. Lucky girl."

*

On the last day of school before vacation, Mort stepped into Nina's classroom to wish the children, and their teacher, a happy holiday. They returned the greeting. Then he was gone.

# 6

# HIATUS

NINA felt as if the basket of the balloon in which she was riding had been cut free of sandbags: she soared. Two weeks of liberation from the threat-promise that Mort and she must interact were hers. As she went about her Christmas shopping, strangers continued to stare at her on the street, as they had been doing recently, and intermittently men cruised her with expressions of such yearning that she hurt for them. What did they discern in her face that called up in them that painful mixture of need and hope? Their loneliness was heightened by the season. Nina gained the sense of a city full of hard-working, mostly successful men, inside of whom hid expectant lovers, who believed (despite the skepticism and heartlessness that their business lives required of them) that somewhere out there lurked a woman who could receive and reciprocate their love and confessions of deep secrets and extravagant dreams. "Is it you?" their eyes asked her. Her gaze flicked away from theirs, not cold, but closed: "No."

She passed the Pulitzer Fountain, and as she paused to admire once again its scale and grace, a tall man, with a sweet countenance and an expensive topcoat, said to her, "May I buy you a fountain?"

Surprised, she smiled up at him. "No, thank you."

Encouraged, he fell into step beside her. "If you're meeting someone . . ."

"My husband," she lied.

"I hope he deserves you."

"Me, too."

They grinned at one another. It was all right. It was enough.

Dear old Manhattan. Nina loved it most because it was home to New Yorkers. Of course, that man might live in Connecticut, but he would never behave that way in Connecticut.

In Bergdorf Goodman, Nina caught sight of herself in a mirror. She tossed off the hood of her raccoon coat. "I'm pretty. I've never looked so glowing and fresh."

Watching a grey-haired clerk write up her charged purchases on a white and lavender sales pad, she considered the changes in herself. "It's love," she decided. "Love is in my face. I see it. Passing strangers see it. Men are drawn to the openness and joy. What does David see? Perhaps David doesn't dare to look."

Far from missing Mort, she reveled in the breathing space the holiday gave them. Everything was enhanced for her because he existed. People seemed uncommonly sympathetic, the city looked spectacular, the golden-pink sunsets over New Jersey, as seen from her apartment, were gems. She laughed at herself and plunged on through the week.

The boys asked for every toy advertised on television between Thanksgiving and Christmas. They would each receive whichever one of these their mother found least obnoxious or easiest to locate. She proceeded to buy unadvertised items that she believed might engage them for more than a few minutes or days: puzzles, games, books, records, clay, and robots with interchangeable parts that could convert into monsters or space ships, depending on how they were assembled. This year each boy was also to receive an Instamatic camera. Nina debated about the appropriateness of stuffed animals for boys and compromised by buying soft little monkeys to peer over the tops of their stockings, rather than the large, huggable fur friends that they would have loved and that she would have chosen for daughters.

David was a more evasive target. This year, most particularly, she wanted her gifts to be inspired. David never hinted at what he wanted, because he regarded present-giving as a test. Each birthday, anniversary, and Christmas, Nina had the impression that he was silently assigning points to the gifts he unwrapped and totaling them for her final score. Whatever enthusiasm her offerings touched off was classified information. He was, as far as she knew, incapable of the sort of emotional display of gratitude and pleasure with which she had grown up and of which Nick Palladino was a master, whether or not he got what he wanted. David's austere upbringing did not make room for displays of any emotion save anger—anger he vented with an unrestraint tantamount to self-indulgence. This was part of his concept of masculinity, and Nina was sure there must be women who agreed with him. She merely felt cheated. Birthdays and Christmases had been more fun with Nick, but as she reminded herself whenever she became nostalgic, as she invariably did, grappling with the letdown of holidays with David, "Life is more than birthdays and Christmas."

What manner of gift receiver was Mort? What would he choose to give her? She fingered wistfully the Christmas card wishing him and Kitty the season's best, from herself and David, and mailed it separately from the others. "Silly," she murmured, standing beside the mailbox. She went blank trying to conjure an image of the gift she would give Mort, were she allowed, but she recognized it at once when she spotted it in the window of an antique store on Madison Avenue: a silver inkstand of superior craftsmanship, with a wafer-box and perforated pounce-box, as well as an inkwell. "How at home it would be on that huge desk in Mort's office," she mused. "But back to the real world: David."

She had bought him more than enough for Christmas morning, but one errand for him was still to be done. David was a confirmed pipe smoker and had a select collection of pipes at home. His pipes and their accessories were of the finest quality, and Nina savored the smell of his choice tobaccos. The few pipes he kept at the office, however, were not of the first rank. Nina had given him a superb one, tagged, "for the office," but he left it at home. He did not like it when she pointed out to him that, considering his eight A.M. to six-thirty P.M. office hours and frequent business trips, most of his smoking hours were spent away from home. He saw in the observation an implied criticism of his priorities, an insinuation, perhaps, that he was a workaholic, who sacrificed his humanity to his ambition. Nina hoped that she had not meant it that way.

She had an ingenious idea. She had heard about a pipe store in Greenwich Village, whose owner hand made briar pipes. She hied herself down there on the subway and located the address she had noted on a cocktail napkin. The shop was warm and aromatic. She chose a well-aged briar pipe, with a large bowl and straight grain; it was handmade and devoid of stain, varnish, or paint. She pictured over and over again David's expression of surprise and approval when he held it for the first time. She was not to witness the happy scene, because she had deduced that the only way for David to have a superior pipe at the office was for her to send it to him there. Since the small pipe store did not deliver, Nina enlisted the aid of David's secretary, who sent a messenger for it (and the pouch of the pipemaker's own tobacco blend, which Nina included). The secretary promised to have the red and green package centered on David's desk when he returned from lunch.

Nina happened to be at home that afternoon, and she rather hoped that David would call to express his gratification, but when the phone rang, it was only another mother, arranging a play date between her son and Gregory. That evening, David was chipper and affectionate but did not comment on the pipe. Nina's determination not to mention it first was defeated by her suspense about his reaction, and she humbled herself with, "Did you get a package from me today?"

David's face tensed and he said self-consciously, "The pipe! It's fine. Sweet, cool smoke."

"It's handmade."

"It's first-rate.

"Does it really smoke better because it's unvarnished and unstained, just the natural, aged briar?" she prompted, disliking herself as she did so.

"Much."

That was all. *Finis*, no applause. She managed not to inquire about the specially blended tobacco. Why had he not brought up her gift? Had the card been lost? Had he thought it might be from someone else? Did he have a mistress? Or in this situation was taciturnity the only possibility left to him, after years of practising it? The familiar disappointment took hold of Nina. For five minutes she wanted to kill him and imagined plunging an ax into his chest. Struggling against the self-wounding penchant for revenge, she defused it with a daydream revolving around her presentation of the silver inkstand to Mort, who was tenderly, merrily grateful and without inhibition in communicating his delight.

From years of living together, Nina picked up David's aware-

ness that, unlike previous, similar occasions, this one did not
feature Nina sunk in self-pity. Within the quarter hour, she had
clearly recovered and was reading *Tom Sawyer* to Gregory and
Zachary. David was very nice to her for the rest of the evening,
and they made love that night with fervor.

The next day, as the Lathrops drove to the country to spend
Christmas there, Nina wondered at her own sincere duplicity. It
had been easy, an established habit, to make love with David, and
she had needed it. Mort-scenes intruded on her interior movie,
but she had learned to enjoy semisurrogate sex. She was not going
to reject her feelings for either man. She was not simply David's
wife, and she was certainly not Mort's mistress. When a creature
is no longer caterpillar and not yet butterfly, does it puzzle over
its indefinite state?

David always drove whenever he was in the car, which irritated Nina, but never enough to upset the children with an
argument. If she had had a girl, she would have had to take a stand
as a role model. Staring out the window, Nina realized that since
Mort had held her hand, she would no longer try to end her
entanglement with him, were she able. The better alternative was
to use her new self-knowledge and sharpened emotional capacity
to improve her marriage to David. She honestly believed, speed-
ing to Connecticut in the midst of her little family, that this was
possible.

\*

Gregory and Zachary were still young enough to have the family up and assembled around the tree at an uncivilized hour on Christmas morning. As their parents drank coffee, they ripped colorful paper from package after package. When a box had Nina's or David's name on it, they handed it over politely but without curiosity and returned to their single-minded concentration on their own haul. Nina's first gift from David was a pair of gold earrings. She shut off the screech of protest and said dutifully, "Thank you, darling."

Where had his mind been when she delivered an articulate, plainly pronounced monologue, the gist of which was that she had more earrings than she wore and did not, thanks all the same, want another pair for Christmas?

"He never *sees* me," she thought furiously. "He never *pays attention.* He was buying the obligatory earrings for his secretaries and receptionist, as usual, and automatically he again lumped me in with his other 'girls.' He himself buys those employees their earrings, plus a pair for me, and then he sends his executive secretary to purchase the rest of his list of presents for me. To David, I'm another personnel problem."

Had David been paying attention, he might have noticed a certain tightness around Nina's eyes, but beyond that, her Christmas morning mask did not betray her. David's secretary had shown taste in running down his list for his wife, and Nina's other presents were admirable. Incensed as she was, Nina's sense of humor cooled her off, and she reflected impishly that running away with Mort was a foolproof way of shutting off the endless flow of secretarial earrings (she never wore them, and David never noticed).

Christmas with Nick Palladino had been gayer but had had its painful aspects, too. She recalled later, as she worked in the kitchen, that he bought for her three or four exquisite treasures and expected her to react like a pampered courtesan. She would have, too (they were always pefect), if they had been paid for. As it was, he had the extravagant fun of shopping for her, then charged everything and let her cope with the bills. She kept their checkbook, and it was summer before she had paid off their creditors for her own Christmas presents. Since he thought it tactless to give her the charge slips, each bill arrived as a surprise, a sickening blow, unfailingly more than she had guessed and requiring the sort of financial sleight of hand that gave her head-aches. He was paying alimony and child support, and their com-bined incomes were never enough to prevent debt.

Remembering, Nina smiled softly. She was wearing a gold ring, set with garnets, which Nick had found for her in an antique store, for their first Christmas together. She loved the ring, but she recalled the stomach cramps that the Master Charge bill had caused her, when she first opened it and for many moons there-after. Nick had never seen the bill, he saw only the ring. The ring was covered with stuffing at the moment and would have to be cleaned.

She trussed the large turkey and shoved it into the hot oven, not missing the housekeeper, who celebrated Christmas at her sister's. The ritual was familiar, and despite its conflicts, it worked —Christmas in the country. The boys had had a happy morning, and Christmas is for children. The Lathrops had their own cycles and traditions, and Nina depended on their rhythm. She was conscious of wanting to hold fast to their security.

Outside the kitchen window, Gregory and Zachary were making a snowman. David contributed an old hat and pipe, and Nina gave them a neckscarf for which they had given her a replacement. The brothers eagerly snapped their progress with their new cameras. If Nina went off with Mort (which she was not going to do), either David or she would be separated from their sons at Christmas. Unbearable. No doubt Mort and Kitty felt the same way about Gillian and Tessa. "I have so much to lose," echoed in Nina's mind.

Walking alone in the woods on the last afternoon before they returned to New York, she decided that if she thought of herself as "in love with" Mort, that translated as "serious; implies future, as well as present, commitment," but if she admitted only to an "infatuation," that translated, "not serious; will pass away." She would love Mort as friend and colleague, realizing that his appreciation of her healed more wounds than she had known she possessed. She would continue, simultaneously, to love David as a satisfactory husband and a good father. Nina halted, breathing lightly, at the sight of a deer pulling bark from a tree with its teeth. She had never become inured to the magic of the animal's sweetness and delicacy. When it moved off through the woods, she turned toward home.

# 7

## BEGINNINGS

NINA opened the front door and threw wide her arms. "Nicole!"

They embraced and kissed.

"You're beautiful."

Nicole beamed and picked up her suitcase. "You look terrific yourself."

"Your room is this way. How was your flight?"

"Noisy. There was a baby in the seat behind me."

Nina led Nicole to the den. "I've made space in the closet and there are empty drawers in the chest."

"Thanks. This is great."

"It's not the Plaza."

"It's better. Where are Zach and Greg?"

"Playing with friends. They'll be home for dinner. As will David, naturally. How's Nick?"

"Dad's fine. He sends his love."

They chatted while Nicole unpacked. She wore jeans, a white turtleneck sweater, and tan boots. Her thick, streaked blonde hair hung down her back, and her face was tanned and glowing.

"Let's go into the living room," Nina suggested when Nicole's gear was stashed away.

They sat side by side on the sofa, and Coral brought them a tea tray, with buttered scones fresh from the oven. They felt cozy and close. During the two and a half years that Nina and Nick were married, Nicole had spent weekends and summers living with them. Although she was only six when they divorced, she was old enough to have grown firmly attached to her stepmother. They corresponded, and on the few occasions when Nick and his third wife brought her to New York, Nicole sought out Nina. It had been several years since their last meeting.

"You're a woman now," said Nina, studying her.

"You sound a little sad about it."

"I was reading my diary not long ago, the one I kept when I was a couple of years younger than you are. I remember how much I expected from life."

"That you didn't get?"

Nina narrowed her eyes and frowned. "I don't know yet."

Nicole looked as if she thought thirty-nine a little long in the tooth still to be waiting.

Nina laughed. "My life is dandy. But the surprises are the best part."

Nicole blurted, before she had time to stop herself, "There's a new man in your life!"

Nina was dumbfounded. She automatically looked toward the door to see if Coral were within hearing distance. For an instant, she considered confessing, but instead she said, with a soupçon of self-mockery, "You'll be a dynamite lawyer, with your eye for detail."

Nicole made a face, disappointed but amenable, not wanting to hear a confidence that would be regretted later.

"How did you choose law?"

"It's an avenue to politics." Nicole elaborated, and she and

Nina were still talking when they heard David's key in the lock. He and Nicole had never met, and he was instantly beguiled by her breezy Western beauty and openness and by her intelligence. Then the boys came home, Coral having picked them up at the apartments of the friends with whom they had spent the day. They, too, were smitten by Nicole, and they all had a lively supper and stayed up past their bedtimes.

\*

The week that followed seemed to pass quickly. Although Nina and Nicole shopped and visited museums, Nicole spent more time at David's office than Nina had anticipated, and Nina admitted to herself (and tried to disguise from them) that she was jealous. Did Nicole assume that Nina was having an affair and that that made David fair game? If so, was she correct? Emotionally, Nina's answer was an explosive No! Intellectually, she saw that an argument could be made. Her ambivalence created a gulf between herself and both David and Nicole and united them. By New Year's Eve, the tension was undeniable. What made it worse for Nina was that she suspected that Mort and Kitty might be at the same party that they were to attend.

A member of Twickham's board of directors and his wife had invited the Lathrops to their New Year's Eve celebration, not because Nina taught there, but because he and David had both served on a fund-raising committee for the school and had solidified their relationship by doing business together. Nina had canvassed the faculty and found that none of the others had been invited, but she did not ask Mort.

Nina, David, and Nicole arrived at the party at ten. There were Mort and Kitty, standing in the foyer of the large Park Avenue apartment, talking to the hostess and drinking champagne. It was a black-tie affair and Mort looked, to Nina's eyes, gorgeous. He smiled at her, but she stood transfixed and expressionless and he looked away. Nina felt Nicole's light tug at her elbow. The host was greeting them, and his wife excused herself from the Hinkses, to join him. Nina responded by rote and went into the purple and white master bedroom, ostensibly to comb her hair. Nicole was right behind her.

"*Who is he?*" she whispered.

"You lawyers," said Nina in exasperation, standing in front of the art nouveau dressing table's mirror.

"C'mon, Nina."

"He's the new headmaster of Twickham. I'll introduce you." Nina checked her image in the mirror and swept from the room head high, lips pursed.

David and Kitty were already sitting on a Victorian love seat, absorbed in conversation—probably about the current exhibit of her paintings. Nina watched them for a moment, fascinated by the picture they made. David, whom she had always characterized as tall, dark, and handsome, looked like a model in an advertisement for the very best Scotch, while Kitty looked piquant and slightly French, like a model in a perfume advert. Her blonde hair (darker than Nicole's streaked mane) grazed bare shoulders, and her long black dress was expertly cut to reveal a slender body without detracting from her air of refinement. Dangling into her modest but inviting cleavage was a golden pendant, free form and set with baroque pearls; it was obviously handmade, the sort of ornament its creator (Kitty herself?) probably termed "body sculpture" rather than "jewelry." Visually arresting, Kitty and David posed with a suggestion of feline suppleness and alertness. Nina hoped that they would not linger like that.

Nina was not wearing a bra, but her scarlet velvet dress did not expose erect nipples as frankly as did Kitty's silky knit. Nina's sweetheart neckline was trimmed with real lace. She had found the gown in one of those boutiques selling old clothes at modern prices. It looked as if its previous owner had never worn it. Nina had tied a black velvet ribbon around her neck and pinned a small, white porcelain camelia to it. She wore her contact lenses instead of glasses. Nicole had told her she looked blazingly romantic.

"You're smashing." Mort was beside her.

She was glad that she had worn low-heeled shoes (just in case), since he was shorter than she.

"Thank you. So are you." She turned to Nicole, luscious in white. "This is Mort Hinks, the headmaster of Twickham. And this, Mort, is my former stepdaughter, Nicole Palladino, who is visiting us from California."

Mort computed the relationship rapidly and shook Nicole's hand. Nina disliked herself for examining his response for attraction to Nicole. He was charming to her but nothing more. Nicole drifted off to join the hosts' eldest daughter and her friends.

"How was your vacation?" Mort asked Nina.

She had drunk rather more champagne than she ought, in such a brief time, and evading the net of small talk he attempted to cast, expounded on her relationship with Nicole and, by association, with Nick. Mort had been treated to a synopsis of her first marriage by the time other guests joined and separated them. Nina was not, in retrospect, as appalled by her confessionary loquaciousness as she might have been, but she did switch to Perrier water for a while.

Soon it was midnight, and David was kissing her. Nicole materialized and kissed first Nina and then David. Nina was, inexplicably, disappointed by the fatherly brushing of lips that her husband bestowed on their nubile young friend. People milled around in slow motion, wishing one another a happy new year, smiling and kissing. A few of the women kissed one another, as well as the men, on the lips, rather than on the cheeks. Nina moved from face to face, from mouth to mouth, smiling, wondering where Mort was and not able to see him.

She turned to say something to David and saw Kitty walk into his arms. They kissed for a few seconds too long with their lips parted a few millimeters too much. Mort stood watching them, his face reflecting such a complex response that although Nina felt she understood it, she was unable to analyze it and labeled it "inscrutable."

Mort caught her gazing at him. He stepped forward and put his hands on the tops of her arms, pinning them to her sides. His two kisses fell on each of her cheeks, in the European manner, and she kissed the air beside his face, unable to reach his flesh. She was congested with disappointment that he had not kissed her on the mouth and exaltation that he had kissed her at all. He did not trust himself to approach her lips, but he raised his champagne glass to her, and as she clinked hers against it, he winked. She winked back.

Nina headed blindly for the bathroom, needing to be alone. Locking herself in, she repaired her image, refreshing eye shadow, powder, and red lip gloss, combing her hair (yanking out a couple of grey strands), and spritzing on perfume. When she had calmed sufficiently, she started back toward the living room. In the dark, candlelit foyer, stood Mort. They were alone. She stopped, wanting him to touch her and terrified that he would. Mort moved to her and put his arms around her. Their lips touched. Lazer lights dispersed and condensed, transluscent, shifting sweeps of color, radiating heat and music, as their lips lingered, withdrew tentatively, melded, and finally opened: his tongue was satiny and warm, it was her mother's nipple when she was an infant, it was his own penis, it was life. She pushed her pelvis against his groin.

"Cool it, you guys," a lyric voice said with as much sweetness as authority.

They split apart and stared at Nicole, like deer caught in the headlights of a car. She put her strong, young arm around Nina's waist. Nina reached up and wiped red lip gloss from Mort's mouth with her fingers. He kissed them lightly, then looked at Nicole, assessing her. Nicole conveyed through the expression on her tanned, beautiful face, the set of her head, a slight movement of her shoulders, that although he was old enough to be her father, she was perhaps less of a novice than he in confronting the perplexities of the human heart and groin. Mort's eyes shone and he saluted her with an oddly gallant gesture of his right hand. He retreated to the living room.

Nicole guided Nina away to the master bedroom, where Nina sat down on the bed. She felt as if she were going to burst into jeweled fragments: diamonds dazzling to the eye, rubies searing against the skin, emeralds sweet upon the taste buds, sapphires purling in the ear, and gold dust everywhere, filling the nostrils with spicy scent.

"Hey, honey, are you going to be all right?" asked Nicole, rubbing her back.

Nina looked into her concerned, encouraging brown eyes and floated up to them, back into familiar air. She took several deep breaths and stood up. "Thanks, Nicole. You saved our life."

Nicole shrugged and smiled.

"I'll find David. I've got to go home," said Nina.

"Do you want me to get him?"

"I'm fine."

*

On New Year's Day, while David watched football on television and Coral took the boys to a movie, Nina and Nicole snuggled down into opposite corners of the living room sofa to talk. They had mugs of coffee and slices of Coral's fruitcake.

"Thank God you were there," said Nina soberly, shaking her head at the prospect of what might have occurred early that morning.

"I don't really know what I walked into," replied Nicole tactfully, giving Nina an opportunity to talk, without pressuring her.

"It was the first time we ever kissed."

"I thought maybe . . ."

"We were having an affair?"

"Mmhhmm."

"No . . . yes . . . not . . . well . . ." She was tongue tied.

"It's not genital?"

"Right."

Silence. Genitals are easier to mention than love.

"Okay, Nicole, look. We . . . I . . . I . . . we . . . oh shit. We do love each other. We've never said so."

"I guess that's wonderful. Love is always . . ."

"A blessing? A special grace? Corny?"

"Except . . ."

"What about David? Greg and Zach?"

Nicole's brown eyes did not judge or dissemble. Nina looked down at her own hands lying in her lap; with her right hand she turned her gold wedding band around and around on its finger.

"Mort and Kitty have two teenage girls," she said.

"You've been divorced before."

"Your father and I didn't have children. Much as I loved you, your own mother was taking good care of you, so I hadn't that responsibility."

Samantha, the Lathrops' orange and white cat, jumped into Nicole's lap and curled up. Nicole stroked her. "How do you feel about David?"

"I'm fond of him. I feel all those ties of time, shared experiences, habit." Nicole's expression caused her to add, "You're too young to realize how strong those can be." Nicole remained dubious. "You'll find out. Anyway, I feel sick imagining where all this can lead. I like my life. I like my husband. I like our family. I like my job. Hell, I'm a disaster area."

Nicole smiled. "Of course you are."

"You have no idea how much I did not want to fall in love, how hard Mort and I tried not to." She told Nicole their tale. The young woman listened with the same quality of attention she had shown when she was five and Nina read aloud to her.

When Nina was finished, Nicole said wistfully, "I don't envy you the complications, but in a way, I'm jealous. Tony and I are sleeping together, but it's no grand passion. It's not fair." She was twisting her golden hair on the back of her head, combing it out with her fingers, braiding it.

"Life isn't fair. You're twenty. You're supposed to be the one this is happening to."

"I wish I were!"

*"So do I."*

"You'd give up Mort?"

"Not anymore. You know, it's not the 'grand passion' that's irresistible. It's the intimacy, the sense of being clearly visible. We see each other, we understand each other, I feel what he feels, he picks up on my emotions instantly. We pay attention to each other."

"You're not lonely anymore."

Nina squinted and held her breath.

"You've always seemed so lonely to me, somewhere deep inside yourself. Now you don't. I noticed it as soon as I arrived."

Nina did not reply.

"I remember telling Daddy, when I was little, that you were like Sleeping Beauty and he'd never hacked through the thorny hedge to you. I guess David didn't, either."

"David has no interest whatsoever in intimacy."

"Lots of people are like that."

"He's satisfied with a friendly, moderately sexy relationship, centered around making a convenient nest. He wants me to be The Wife and to fulfill that social role, but he hasn't a clue about how I feel or respond. Except in bed."

"Could be worse."

"Could be better."

"And is?" Nicole carefully picked all the candied cherries out of her slice of fruitcake.

"Overwhelming. Communication doesn't matter to David, but he's sensed I'm changing somehow, and he tries almost to woo me. It's strange. He's more thoughtful, kinder and everything, but I feel as if it comes not from his caring but from his deciding that that behavior on his part will produce the desired results in me. As if I could respond to manipulative behavior the same way I do to genuine candor and concern. What I respond to is the manipulation behind the thoughtfulness, not to the thoughtfulness, but David doesn't even see that. If I'm pleasant and warm, he thinks he's succeeded. He doesn't notice that the exchange has been bloodless. It's very lonely. You're right. Living with a facade."

"In a way he is being genuine. He cares enough to try."

"Did you know poinsettia leaves are fatal if eaten?" Nina crinkled the decorative foil on the red and green plant's pot, which sat on the end table.

"Yes."

"David cares about preserving the status quo, keeping the family together, not being rejected. So do I. But lying can't do that any more."

"He lies to you?"

"Manipulation is lying. And he has all these surrogate relationships with women he works with. He thinks I don't know because he's circumspect. The deceit alienates me more than the betrayal."

"You see his working relationships with other women as betrayals?"

"Don't be silly. I'm not nuts. Most of them, no, but a few."

"And particularly Emily?"

"Hah! You noticed!"

"She's a junior partner in his firm. She's black, and black is beautiful. They spend a great deal of time together."

"More than he spends really being with me. They're more truly intimate than he and I are."

Nicole looked out the window at the bare treetops. The Lothrops' fourth-floor apartment was less expensive than those on higher floors; but street noises were audible and bothersome.

"Well?"

"Yes, Nina, that was my impression. I don't think they've been to bed or anything."

"I don't care. Before Emily, it was someone else. It's always someone. Else. David shares more thoughts and feelings with her than with me. When it's only a passing physical thing (that happens, too), it hurts me in a different way. If I find out about it. David and Emily, or whoever is playing that part for him, keep the illusion of their romantic potential by not doing anything. Titillation. Love has nothing to do with it. Portia complains that Brutus keeps her in the suburbs of his life. Well, David exiles me to exurbia. He commutes to me for sex. I'm his bedroom community. We outline our days for each other, leaving out how we felt and whom we cared about. I don't know, it's so superficial and dishonest."

An ambulance screamed in the street below. When the sound had faded, Nicole said, "No wonder you're vulnerable to Mort. Why do you stay married?"

"I've only painted the dark side. We have good times. David is one of the most interesting men I've ever known. We function well together as parents. Our life-style suits us. It all runs smoothly and pleasantly enough. We have strong bonds I couldn't describe. I love him, but living with him is lonely."

"You're jealous with David. Are you with Mort?"

"Not at all. Isn't that wild? I'm not even jealous of his wife. But I'm aware of how he reacts to other women. I do notice."

"You must be very sure of him."

"And not of David? Maybe. I suspected you and David."

Nicole laughed. "I know. I thought it was paranoid, but I

guess it was wishful thinking. You'd feel less guilty about Mort if David had a new lady."

"I don't think he'd marry Emily."

"He seemed more sincerely interested in Mort's wife— what's her name—than in any of the women he works with."

"Kitty? I agree. She paints as Catherine Myers, and David is a fan."

Nicole did not say what she was thinking.

"They looked beautiful together," Nina said for her.

"You sound dejected."

"I know Mort and I aren't a beautiful couple."

"I think you are."

Samantha left Nicole's lap, stretched, and removed herself to the top of a radiator.

"You're a dear. But we have no glamour. I'll never forget the way Kitty and David looked, both dressed in black, talking on that love seat. Kissing at midnight."

"Maybe David is suspicious of you and Mort and was getting back at you, by coming on to Kitty."

"I doubt it. But even so, they weren't acting."

"David is sexy. He's too slick for me, but women stare at him on the street. He's smart and probably rich."

"We've put more money into investments than we've spent on ourselves, but his firm has acquired a communications con-glomerate. It's their first fantastically major client and we're going to be loaded. It'll change our whole life."

"There are women who are more turned on by his success trip than you are."

Nina, who had been sitting Indian fashion on the plump green sofa pillow, uncrossed her legs and planted both feet on the floor. "David and I aren't going to split. This is crazy. We're speculating."

"Which is how fortunes are made."

Nina laughed. "Happy New Year, toots."

Nicole raised her coffee mug, sipped thoughtfully, and said, "Good fortune to us all."

\*

Before she left, Nicole bought four gift records.

For Gregory and Zachary: Mel Brooks. The boys had been regaled by every movie he, Marty Feldman, and Gene Wilder had made and had described their favorite routines for her amidst much laughter.

For David: Bobby Short singing Cole Porter. One evening, David had taken Nina, Nicole, and the twenty-one-year-old son of one of his law partners to the Café Carlyle, where they had become happily high on Dom Perignon and on the romantic dream that that superb performer expresses with such incomparable finesse and sophistication.

For Nina: *Albert Finney's Album.* "But he's a movie star," she thought, puzzled until she played it. Finney sang the words he had written, but Nina heard Mort.

> The gentle warmth of your caress,
> You didn't learn that yesterday,
> The joy I have in your embrace,
> Because your body knows the way.

. . . I love you for what you are,
Composed of all that you have seen,
As you are now, not might have been,
So don't disown
The loves you've known.

And for both Nina and David: a Patti Smith album. "So you don't forget this is the 'seventies," Nicole explained. Then she was gone.

# 8

## SHORT TAKES

"WHY me?" Nina kept asking herself. "Why am I, secure with David in our oasis but surrounded by parched desert wanderers, the one who's getting rained on?"

*

*Nina is lunching with Karen, her former college roommate, at a delicatessen near Twickham.*

KAREN: Mark's a good husband. I love him. Our life suits us. But it's dull, you know what I mean?

NINA: You've been married for fifteen years. What do you expect?

KAREN: I still daydream about Bob sometimes.

NINA: He was a poet. You can't marry poets.

KAREN: He was so intense about everything.

NINA: And irresponsible.

KAREN: I look up his name in the phone book whenever a new one comes out. He's never there. He's not in Manhattan.

NINA: Or he's unlisted.

KAREN: Walking down the street, I search for his face. Sometimes I think for a moment I see him. My heart races.

\*

*Cal has stopped by for a drink with the Lathrops on the way home from his office.*

CAL: If you two ever think about splitting, take it from me, don't.

NINA: You were the one who wanted to divorce Joan.

CAL: It's grim living alone. I even miss the kids' fights and their toys all over the living room.

DAVID: You're out every night.

CAL: Singles bars! All those girls want is one-night stands. I got fed up with that scene in six months. I feel as if I should collect stud fees.

NINA: What do you want then?

CAL: I want that old cliché, a meaningful relationship.

\*

*Nina and Peggy are sitting on a bench in Twickham's rooftop playground, watching their classes during recess.*

PEGGY: Remember my telling you about Sally, my friend who

didn't marry until she was thirty-three and then had twins, seven months later?

NINA: That was years ago.

PEGGY: Only four. Her husband is a nice guy. He loves her.

NINA: Doesn't she love him?

PEGGY: She says she does, but she's screwing around. Says the thrill is gone, with her husband.

NINA: What else is new? Who takes care of the twins, while she's cavorting?

PEGGY: She has live-in help. She's a freelance illustrator, so she's always meeting art directors, editors, and writers.

NINA: She screws them all?

PEGGY: Nearly. Once or twice. Then she drops them because they don't have it. I was afraid she'd wreck her career and her marriage, but her husband refuses to see, and she uses her marriage as an excuse with her lovers. She says she feels too guilty and breaks it off.

NINA: Her lovers buy that?

PEGGY: Who wants to face being a lousy lay?

NINA: They all are? Maybe she's in the wrong business.

PEGGY: She's going after that sexual obsession of the first few months, but no one excites her enough.

NINA: She sounds jaded.

\*

*Nina and Pam, a weekend guest, are sunbathing on the deck of the Lathrops' converted barn in Connecticut.*

PAM: You like being married, don't you?

NINA: I'm the type. Do you think you ever will?

PAM: Probably not. Jack's reliable. We've been together for ages, but I have my own flat.

NINA: To have everything your own way? Has its appeal.

PAM: That, and for when I want to bring another man home.

NINA: Does Jack know you have other men?

PAM: We don't discuss it.

NINA: It looks as if you have your cake and (you should excuse the expression) eat it, too.

PAM: That's the theory. But lately I can't find a lover. There's Jack and more Jack. Period. For over a year. Do you think I'm over the hill?

NINA: Dummy. Are you meeting men you want who don't want you?

PAM: Nothing. *Nada. Niente. Rien.*

\*

*Nina is talking to Gretchen, at a dinner party.*

GRETCHEN: Do you think the man they asked here for me is gay?

NINA: Why would they do that?

GRETCHEN: Why not? Every man I've met since I was divorced is gay.

NINA: That's not possible.

GRETCHEN: Gay. Or married.

NINA: Gays turn bisexual and married men get divorced. Where's your fighting spirit?

GRETCHEN: None of my gay friends wants to try bisexuality. The married men want affairs they can squeeze into their busy schedules without alerting their wives.

NINA: So what do you do?

GRETCHEN: See gays for companionship and married men for lunchtime and early-evening sex.

NINA: Sounds schizophrenic.

GRETCHEN: I wish I could get it all together. One man of my own is all I ask. One. Is that unreasonable?

\*

*Nina and David are having a drink during the intermission of a concert.*

DAVID: Jerry said today he's beset with marriage proposals.

NINA: Lucky Jerry.

DAVID: To the contrary. These are ladies with small children, looking for a husband-daddy to restore them to nuclear family status.

NINA: What's wrong with that?

DAVID: They're depressingly practical about the whole thing. And there are the businesswomen who want husbands, to enhance their careers. They need escorts.

NINA: What are they offering as their part of the bargain?

DAVID: The *quid pro quo* is their companionship, convenient sex, and an organized home and social life. Stability.

NINA: Poor Jerry. He's a dear.

DAVID: He wants to love and be loved.

NINA: Don't we all.

# 9

### CAPITULATION

CONTEMPLATING her return to Twickham and confrontation of Mort, Nina felt as if her intestines were disintegrating into overcooked spaghetti—sodden, slippery, and limp. She was afraid that if she saw Mort, she would embarrass herself and him by trembling, stammering, blushing, and possibly fainting away at his feet. She lectured herself about keeping her cool. She prayed for self-control. She willed her actions to appear normal. By lunchtime of the first day after vacation, she needed a drink but restrained herself. After school, she hid in her classroom, planning to stay so late that there would be no chance of meeting Mort. When the door opened, she strove to keep her face neutral. It was Beverly, Mort's secretary, bundled up in her winter coat.

"Dr. Hinks asked me to drop by on my way out and see if you were still here. He'd like to see you before you go."

"Thanks, Beverly. I was just going to leave," she lied. "Be careful. The sidewalks are icy and your center of gravity has shifted."

"I know. I walk slowly. I can hardly get my coat buttoned over the baby these days."

Nina collected her coat and bag and marched herself to Mort's office. He was going to fire her. This was it. The ax. The end. ("I'm sure you can understand, Ms. Lathrop, that under the circumstances . . .") Except for noisy pockets of extracurricular activities, the building was deserted. Beverly's office was dark. Nina went in and shut the hall door behind her. She knocked on the inner door.

Mort's voice was strong. "Come in."

She entered, closed that door, and leaned against it. Her lips quivered. She could not do it. She was unable to act the brave, confident, spunky part she had scripted in her head.

Mort stood up. "Come on in. Sit down." He stepped around his desk and indicated the brown leather couch under the window. The blinds were drawn. His face was so sensitive and purposeful that it drew her into the room. They sat down a yard apart.

Mort leaned toward her and said earnestly, "I want to talk to you because I'm sorry about New Year's Eve."

Nina looked stricken. That was worse than being fired.

He responded, "Not the kiss. The indiscretion."

She roused herself and said, "Nicole won't tell anyone."

"I'm sorry to rely on her loyalty in place of my own judgment."

Nina was dazed. He had said, "Not the kiss."

"I can't claim to have been high," he continued, intent upon restoring her good opinion of him, were it in jeopardy. "I'd had a few glasses of champagne. No grass. I was relatively sober." He stopped, searching. "Finding myself alone with you, in the dark, with the candlelight, and you'd been telling me earlier about Nick, and I felt close to you, and I . . . it happened."

She was mute.

"What more can I say?"

Her silence distressed him.

"Don't be sorry about any of it," she pleaded. "Don't."

Motionless, they sank into one another's eyes, and then they were kissing again, slowly, luxuriously, without resistance or effort. The rhythm built, the contrast of warm mouths and cool skin, silky hair and rough, half-day's beard growth, ravishing light and enrapturing darkness. When Mort's hand progressed to Nina's waist and under her sweater, she revived briefly ("This is really happening."). For an interval she felt like a teenager; there were the awkward pause and the dismay that he was able to unfasten her bra with one hand ("He isn't out of practice, or is it a skill once gained, never lost?"). The touch of his fingers on her breasts, which erased dismay and thought. Her amazement when his avid, expert lips on her nipple catapulted her into a shimmering catena of orgasms.

Her protest, then, that things had gone too far: "I'm not on the pill." His reassurance: "I've had a vasectomy." (Later, she smiled over that: her luck was twenty-four carat). They managed the disrupting details of shedding their clothes. No more words. They accelerated and braked, devoured and teased, explored and discovered. They were blissed out. Lost. Found. Shattered. Restored.

"Oh my God," she said, hours or minutes later, when they had returned to time and space. They lay quietly in one another's arms on the leather couch. Mort got up and locked the door.

Nina sat bolt upright. "You mean the door was unlocked?"

"Anyone could have walked in." He was ironic. "Don't you love my penance for indiscretion?"

She choked back her response, not emboldened to say, "I love you."

He understood and said, "I love you, Nina."

She rose and pressed her body against his. "I love you. All of you."

They kissed. She felt his penis stir.

"This man," she thought, "is forty-five years old. I'd better not be greedy." She said, "I should go."

"I know."

Naked and musky, they stood there on the oriental carpet, holding one another, in Mort's wood-paneled office, beside his desk stacked with Twickham correspondence and reports, surrounded by his wife's paintings on every wall: it seemed unreal. They dressed self-consciously, watching one another (Mort wore jockey, not boxer, shorts, and Nina wore no panties with her panty hose). Nina took Kleenex from Beverly's desk and wiped the couch dry.

"You leave first," Mort said, putting his glasses back on. "We can't go home together, because apparently I can't keep my hands off you. I was sure when I asked you here that I was never going to touch you again. I had convinced myself that we could still go back."

She bowed her head and replied without conviction, "Maybe we can."

He tilted up her chin.

"No," she said. "We can't."

He kissed her gently, but contact transformed gentleness into something more robust. With difficulty he straightarmed her and smiled. "Get out of here, before we do something else we ought to regret."

He helped her into her raccoon coat but did not kiss her again.

The next day, in the faculty lounge, Mort carried his coffee over to Nina and sat down beside her on the black vinyl couch. She noticed that his coffee was the same leather-tan color that hers was; she wondered if he took sugar (she did not).

"Can you leave school at five this afternoon?" he asked. "We'll share a cab home, so we can talk."

"Fine."

"If you don't see me in front of school, don't wait there. Meet me in the drugstore on the corner, so it looks accidental."

She smiled at his expertise, and he said defensively, "I'm new at this."

Her smile widened. "So am I. Apparently we have a knack for it."

"Time will tell." He got up and joined a group of male faculty from the upper school.

Nina pretended to be reading, but the words on the page and indeed the alphabet were unrecognizable. Her present survival strategy consisted of getting through small chunks of time successively, not looking beyond the current one. She had concealed her inner trance-state at home the previous evening by striving to remember how she had behaved before she and Mort became lovers and imitating that person. It worked. Deception was necessary, but it saddened her to discover how convincingly she practiced it. All the while, she caroled inwardly, "We're lovers." That she hardly believed it did not make it untrue.

As Nina sat in the lounge, staring at her book but not seeing it, the mental tape that had been playing in a number of versions since the night before rewound and commenced: "Mort is so honorable, so good and reliable a man, that he apologized to me for kissing me indiscreetly. David has never apologized to me for anything, not for yelling insults at me, not for assorted emotional and sexual infidelities, not for ignoring me, not for any of the disagreeable things that have happened. Mort apologized for loving me, 'not wisely but too well.' "

She felt queasy and restless, so unaccustomed was she to being treated with what she perceived as a fine decency.

"You'll wreck it," she warned herself. "If you don't let yourself be loved this way, this time, if you run scared, you'll never have another chance." Panic. "I owe it to David and the boys to retreat. I shall resist Mort. I'll get a job at another school." Relief. "It will be safe, being back where I was, back where I know the way."

Something made her look up. Mort enveloped her with a look that said, "Don't worry about being scared. I'm scared, too. That won't separate us."

Resist Mort? What a quaint idea. She closed her book. Time to get back to class.

Nina did not have enough to keep her busy at school until five, so she shopped on Lexington Avenue before meeting Mort in the drugstore. Mort asked the cab driver to circle Central Park until he was told to stop. It was a Checker cab, and the glass partition was closed, so they had a modicum of space and privacy. A cold rain had begun to fall (as the weatherman had predicted), the light was failing, and they felt secure from being seen and recognized in the park. If they had been spotted getting into the cab, it would be assumed that they were sharing it innocently, since they both lived on the West Side.

When they had driven into the park, Mort held Nina, silently, and finally kissed her, with a tenderness that gave her more pain than joy. No man had ever been so vulnerable with her, and it unnerved her. She wrestled her neurosis to the mat and accepted his gift.

"What do you want to do?" he asked. "About us?"

She reflected. "I want today. I can't think about tomorrow."

"We can't use my office again."

"No, we can't."

"Now is when we have to think about that."

He was having difficulty with this discussion. Her need to help him with it gradually overpowered her avoidance mechanisms.

"If only there were a sanitorium where we could go," she said.

"We're not ill!"

"Still, there should be an idyllic tropical island exclusively for people like us, like a tuberculosis sanitorium where we'd stay . . ."

"And?"

"Talk and make love."

"Yes!"

"Until we were cured, and then we'd carry the memory of that time with us always, like an implanted energy cell."

"Cured?"

"Returned to the realities of everyday life, with our families."

"I was trying to say that a hotel is out, because it's too risky and too expensive."

The cab stopped at a red light. An intrepid jogger sloshed across the road, his orange warm-up suit reflecting in the wet pavement.

Mort's face was boyish as he struggled with the logistics of a place where they were to make love. Nina had thought he wanted to discuss how they might disengage. She had expected to go along as before, loving from a distance, with occasional unexpected surrenders to passion.

"We can't leave it to chance," he said. "That's too dangerous. We have to recognize that we are going to make love and then arrange for that, so it's not accidental and self-destructive."

His mind was working as it did on school problems. She barely managed to ask, "How?"

"Maybe we can rent a one-room walkup somewhere inconspicuous."

"New York is a collection of small towns. Any place near enough to be convenient will be in a neighborhood where there will be people who know us."

"As inconspicuous as possible."

She goaded herself into saying, "Well, actually, I have this friend, Gretchen, who mentioned the other week that an actor friend of hers is going to the coast for four months and wants to sublet his apartment here. But I don't know if he'd rent it for less time, or where it is."

"You expect to be 'cured' in under four months?"

"Under you."

"Flattering."

"Doesn't sound realistic, does it?"

"Four months is the stopgap we need."

They both laughed at his unintentional *double entendre.*

"When is the actor leaving, and what's he charging?"

"I can't recall. Gretchen thought I might know someone who was getting divorced and needed a halfway house, but I don't."

She tensed because she had mentioned the newly taboo word, d-i-v-o-r-c-e.

Mort dismissed the slip. "Will you phone her tonight?"

"I can't tell her it's for us."

"Get her friend's name and phone number, and I'll contact him."

"He'll tell Gretchen it's you."

Mort slumped with discouragement. "You're playing, 'Yes, but . . .'"

"I'll call Gretchen and make her promise not to tell a soul that you're the one who's subletting the place."

"Is she trustworthy?"

"Usually."

Nina looked out the window, speckled with raindrops. An indefatigable dog-walker huddled under a black umbrella, beneath bare, black trees, as his glistening Doberman pulled him into the wind.

"We have to chance it," said Mort.

"Aren't you frightened?"

"Yes. What are you imagining?" He took her hand. "It's permissible to be frightened, you know. Tell me your most awful projection."

"Really? It's . . . here goes . . . that we're discovered, we both lose our jobs, David and Kitty divorce us and get custody of the children by naming you and me, respectively, as corespondents. We're out in the street, unemployed."

"You do race your motor. Are we loveless?"

"Say again?"

"Are we together or apart?"

She examined her fantasy. "Together."

"That's the nightmare?"

Nina was perplexed.

"Ghastly, isn't it?" He kissed her playfully.

"My mind does a doom-and-gloom number, but my heart doesn't believe a word of it."

"You won't lose your boys—or me, unless we're both ready." He kissed her thoroughly. Desire flared and they wrenched apart.

"Damn it," he said.

Nina answered lightly, "We've got to stop meeting like this."

"We've got to stop meeting at all, until we have our own place."

Her sense of unreality became increasingly dense. "Our own place." This was happening to a her with whom she had had slight previous acquaintance. The rain fell more urgently. Inside the taxicab, the air was stuffy and warm. She opened the window on her side a couple of inches.

In an effort to touch solid ground, she asked, "How will we pay our rent without David and Kitty missing the money?" It was hard to say those names. "I have my own savings account, but a withdrawal once a month for a consistent amount looks too suspicious."

"Does David examine your bank book?"

"I doubt it, but he can if he wants. He has access."

"I'll pay the rent from my savings and keep the book at the office."

Nina was startled to hear herself say, "I insist on paying half. I'll withdraw it in irregular amounts throughout the month."

He acceded. "I'll send him, the actor, money orders. Kitty does see my checkbook."

"I can't afford a high rent."

"We don't need a luxury building or vast floor space. Listen,

I'm going to avoid being alone with you until we take an apartment. We'll talk to make arrangements, either with the actor or to find another place, and about school business, but that's all."

"Nothing personal? We'll confine ourselves to our work and our love nest?"

"Nothing more personal than that. I don't want you to think I don't love you, when I seem distant."

"I won't."

"You did after Thanksgiving. We were both polite and casual, and you believed I didn't care."

"I was afraid you'd abandoned me."

"I didn't know what to do." There was anguish in his voice. "I was so torn between wanting you and trying to back off. I never wanted to hurt you."

This time, she initiated their kiss.

When he was able to speak, Mort told the cab driver to drop him off on Central Park West and then to take the lady to West End Avenue. As Nina got out, she left her umbrella in the cab; the awning in front of her building kept her dry, and she did not miss the umbrella until the next rainstorm.

# 10

## NEWNESS

By concentrating studiously, Nina simulated her former self. At home she kept her guilt and sorrow subterranean. Her alliance with Mort affected her family profoundly but not on the surface, for their existence was predicated on deceit (hers) and ignorance (theirs). As a woman probably knows, at a preconscious level, that she is pregnant, before recognizable signs are manifest, so the Lathrops, one and all, must subtly have sensed that they were no longer as they had been.

Nina's dependence on David withered, even as she went through the habitual motions of companionship. Her involvement with her sons shifted perspective, too, for she upgraded her evaluation of their capacities for self-reliance and survival, as she stopped using them to justify having settled for a marital arrangement that was sterile in comparison with the true marriage she had always thought she wanted.

Nina now set her emotional compass by Mort, rather than David, but this time she was on the trail alone. Mort was in the thicket of his family life, she in the copse of hers, and if they met, it was fleetingly, at their secret spring, to lessen their thirst. By February first, when their sublet began, they were parched. They had taken Gretchen's actor-friend's top-floor walkup in an East

Side brownstone. They each had a key. They left the actor's name on the mailbox. Mort had inspected the place, but Nina had not.

The January intermission had given them time to become accustomed to their new identities. In the beginning, Nina awoke next to David, in the morning, and was her old self (low-keyed comfortable) until she began remembering Mort: as a chameleon who, upon discovering that its peregrinations have taken it from rough, rigid bark to the smooth resilient surface of a leaf, changes from somber brown to sprightly green, so Nina lightened and colored. By the end of January, Nina awoke next to David and was her new self immediately: a woman as protective and nurturing of her own nascent gift for passionate intimacy as she had been of her babies' welfare, a woman confident for the first time in her life (and despite merely patronizing concern from the man whose bed she shared) that she was loved, desired, understood, and taken seriously in full measure. She stretched like a cat, gloating, atingle with expectation and apprehension, smiling, sometimes, through the mists of receding dreams.

\*

For their premier rendezvous, Nina arrived at the apartment with a can of coffee, a quart of milk, French bread, an assortment of cheeses and fresh fruits, and Perrier water. In her grocery bag also were paper towel, Kleenex, soap, and detergent.

"It's inescapable," she thought. "The domestic shit. The slow accretion, like barnacles. I'm meeting my lover in our hideaway, and I have an armload of groceries. This can never work."

Mort arrived with a chilled bottle of Louis Roederer Cristal and a bouquet of violets. He had a sense of occasion. Nina was grateful that the champagne was Roederer Cristal, not the more obvious and less lovely Dom Perignon, grateful that the flowers were (at long last) violets, not roses, grateful that the man was Mort, not anyone else.

The apartment was a living-dining room with a fireplace, a small kitchen, a bedroom almost fully occupied by a king-size brass bed, and a small bathroom. It had a closed-in, personal aroma, indefinable but attractive. The actor's. Nina liked him more for his scent than for his style. The furnishings were conventional Sloane/Bloomingdale's modern, with neutral colors, contrasting textures, glass, chrome, and greenery (they had promised to water the plants). Drama was reserved for the midnight blue bedroom, with its giant bed, strategically placed mirrors, and thick carpet; Mort had warned her that it looked like a bordello.

In preparation for this day, Nina had bought a pair of dark sunglasses, unlike any others she had ever owned, and a beret, although she had always avoided berets as unbecoming to her. In a telephone booth near the brownstone, she had ("like Clark Kent") put on the glasses and tucked her brown curls under the beret. When she reached their building, she glanced furtively in every direction before ducking into the doorway. She had put the new keys on her regular key ring, between home-and-car keys and school keys. Trudging up four flights of stairs, seeing only dimly through her dark lenses, she hoped hard that none of her new neighbors would open their doors. On every floor lurked potential witnesses in the spectral divorce-and-custody litigation that Nina felt loured at them.

She had put away the groceries and hung up her coat before Mort got there. Being alone together in an apartment was disorienting. The obstacles that had separated them and so had increased their sexual tension were removed. They were free to do whatever they liked, and by being here, making arrangements, taking risks, they were obligated to like love and sex rather than, as formerly, to resist them. Mort hung up his coat, took off his aviator sunglasses, and put the champagne in the refrigerator. Nina accepted his violets shyly and put them in a glass of water. The two of them stood in the small kitchen, not touching, not having kissed hello.

"Are you hungry?" Nina asked.

"Not really. You?"

Nina shook her head.

They went into the living room and hesitated awkwardly, restrained from lunging at one another both by a sense of decorum and by the numbing of desire that accompanies pressure to perform. They were a couple alone in their own apartment but without ritual or routine, adrift in unfamiliarity. Nina put the violets on the glass coffee table and then turned to Mort, amusement and anxiety in her face. He caressed her cheek. She kissed his palm. The warm vibrancy of skin upon skin restored their sense of purpose. As he picked her up and carried her to the bedroom, she worried that he would strain his back, but she did not say so. Being in bed fulfilled the fantasy. Mort was the uninhibited lover whom Nina had always imagined. The pleasures she was ashamed to suggest to David, she did not need to suggest to Mort, for he needed those satisfactions as urgently as she.

The telephone rang, jarring them.

"I didn't give the number to anyone," said Mort.

"I don't know it," said Nina. "Don't answer. It's for the actor."

In unison they looked at the clock on a shelf by the bed, and their X-rated film became transformed into a speeded-up 'twenties comedy as they raced into their clothes and out the door, Nina leaving first and walking east, Mort leaving a few minutes later and walking west.

\*

Mort established a pattern of working late and pushed his hour of arrival home to seven o'clock. Unaccustomed as he was to lying to his wife, he told Kitty that he did not answer his office telephone because if people discovered he was available after hours, they would interrupt him. He required, he explained, time to read, write, and think, now that Twickham was in the throes of its vigorous annual fund-raising campaign. He was, concomitantly, reordering priorities and reorganizing the curriculum. The volume of work was as great as he claimed, but by working at home and on weekends, rising early and going to bed late, he was able to withstand the stress and still see Nina for an hour or two several days a week. With her, he refueled and retooled.

Sometimes they met at their apartment in the morning. Nina told David that she had joined a gym and was working out before school started. Her sexual athletics improved her muscle tone enough so that he believed her. Sometimes they met at noon, eating in bed, or not eating, making love, or not making love, for there were times when they talked nonstop. On that very first day, they returned after school and drank the champagne and ate warmed, crusty French bread with juicy sweet pears and runny cheese (it had been sitting on the kitchen counter since noon).

Such late-afternoon assignations were more leisurely, they were to discover. Nina invented a clutch of excuses for Coral and David —that she was at the gym, working at school, researching in the library a book she wanted to write on education, seeing friends.

Nina and Mort worked in the apartment, too, sitting together at the Danish-modern dining table or reading on the beige velveteen couch, legs propped up on the glass-and-chrome coffee table. Lascivious as they were, they hungered for one another's conversation and sheer presence as avidly as for one another's tumescence, moisture, odor, heat, strength, and surrender. Nina bought them each slippers and cozy robes to keep in the actor's closet: blue plaid for Mort, amber fleece for herself. They came to regard their place as more authentically home than their family apartments, an alarming development.

\*

"Why did you choose teaching?" Mort asked Nina one Saturday, as they were eating delicatessen sandwiches at their dining room table. Logs were burning in the fireplace.

"Power."

He considered before saying, "But you're not manipulative."

She grinned. "To help children to form a sure sense of their assets and weaknesses, excite them about the real world and finding out about it."

"Modest ambitions." He had finished his roast beef on a roll and was watching her over the rim of his white coffee mug.

"I try to provide the children with space and guidance, so

that it will be hard for anyone to screw them up later," she explained. "If you play to the children's best selves, they'll remember how it feels to be at their best. I keep hoping that most of them will never lose that."

"Sounds more like psychology than teaching."

"Not really." Nina went into the kitchen and got the coffee pot, refilling their mugs. She also brought milk in a little blue pitcher (her mother's voice: "Don't bring the carton to the table.").

"I take them as far as they can go with reading and arithmetic," she continued, "but my most important contribution is firing their enthusiasm for school and learning. School should be fun and even the unpleasant parts, like cleaning up, ought to give them a sense of accomplishment."

"You're such an idealist."

"Impractically so?"

"I guess not."

They took their coffee and sat on the white shag rug in front of the fire.

Mort said, "We all know now that a baby whose crying is not responded to learns that the world is unresponsive. By the time he's five, unless there's been dramatic, caring intervention, that's his view of life, and it's fairly well set. You help them build on the best of whatever they've got at five."

"How did you get into education?"

"Children are the future. I read somewhere that during an international crisis (Bay of Pigs, maybe), when Jack Kennedy gave Caroline short shrift, old Joe Kennedy reprimanded him, saying that the most important thing he'd ever do was to be a parent; it was more important than being president."

"And being headmaster is like being superparent?"

Mort grinned. "I've never thought of it quite that way." He paused and then said deliberately, "Kitty accuses me of hubris."

"What is painting, then?"

"Kitty says painting is ambitious in a smaller, more personal way, that it's primarily expressive."

Nina's fingers tightened on the handle of the mug, and she stared down into the tan liquid. She had wanted to ask him this for weeks, and now it seemed safer to make a statement: "Painting is intrinsically more interesting than teaching."

When he did not reply, she looked up at him. What she saw was devotion to her and aching regret that her self-regard was weak. She wondered if any musical instrument were as responsive as he. Did a guitarist have the same sense of effecting fluid, subtle responses that she had, while talking to Mort? Perhaps playing a Stradivarius was similar.

"Teachers don't get reviewed in newspapers and magazines," she said.

"That reveals more about our society than about teaching. Urie Bronfenbrenner writes that one criterion for judging the worth of a society is 'the concern of one generation for the next.' I guess that's how I judge people, too: by their concern for the next generation."

"Educators aren't the only ones who have that."

"Obviously. Art is a treasure for future generations and all that."

"Do you think future graduate students will be writing about Kitty?"

"Very unlikely. She's voguish. Decorative. She has a finely honed sense of color and design."

"Doesn't she take herself more seriously than that?"

"We all take ourselves seriously."

"History may disagree with you."

"Let's hope so, for Kitty's sake. Personally, I'm excited by people who get more directly involved."

"With children?"

"Especially today, when it's trendy to sell kids short."

Nina was too warm and moved away from the fire, sitting on the rug, with her back against the couch.

Mort said with mock righteousness, "Your reward is your lasting imprint on all those lives."

She made a face at him. "Too theoretical and intangible."

"You're considering a new career?"

"No way."

He lay down with his head in her lap and said, "Painters devote themselves to themselves, their own visions and skills. Teachers devote themselves to others."

"I'm not selfless." She thought, staring into the fire and caressing his grey-blonde hair, "If I were, I wouldn't be here with you."

"Your ego is bigger, in a way. You want the children you teach to be different and better than they'd have been without you. Kitty only asks recognition of who she is and what she sees."

"If I had an original way of seeing things, I'd want to express it, too. Perhaps I'm a teacher by default."

"You're too available emotionally to work in an artist's isolation."

"That's what draws you to me?"

"In part. You're a tough lady."

"Tough?"

"This arrangement isn't easy." He reached up and unbuttoned her blouse.

"The lying is difficult. It's not my style. Nor yours."

"You worry about getting caught." He propped himself up on one elbow and exposed her transparent, front-opening brassiere.

"Anyone might see either of us coming here."

"The faculty, or Kitty and David, may begin to wonder about our absences." He unhooked her bra and folded the cups out of the way.

"I get through each day, that's all. I guess I'm happier than I've ever been, in spite of the problems."

Mort's eyes were on Nina's breasts, and her harem fantasies surfaced: sitting with bared breasts while a fully dressed man carried on a sensible conversation excited her as much as he thought it would.

He said, "You predicted once that we'd be 'cured' of each other."

Her breathing was shallow and quick. "To get free of each other. Sated. Satiated. Saturated."

"Fed up."

They both smiled and she said, "We don't have to go that far."

His eyes made love to her. "Is it working?"

"Hell no!"

He touched her and ended the conversation.

\*

Mort was reading a study of affluent children when Nina arrived late one afternoon in a state of panic.

"I was recognized," she blurted.

He became attentive but not alarmed. "Take it easy, darling."

He helped her out of her raccoon coat and steered her to the brown-and-navy print armchair by the window, standing above her and looking down. "Now, tell me, who and so what?"

"Here. On this block. This man—I've never known his name—who lived in my building while I was a divorcée, he used to be out walking his long-haired dachshund all the time. I mean, he seemed sweet and lonely, and he sort of hung around the neighborhood with his dog. He'd say 'hello' to everyone he recognized from our building. After I married David and moved, I'd run into him once every few years, and we'd smile and say 'hi.' Then I forgot about him. But I've noticed him around here. He's tall and bald and now he walks a Lhaso; his dachshund must've died. I kept meaning to tell you but I forgot. I've tried to avoid him and never show any sign of recognition, but today he was walking past when I got here, and he said, 'We're neighbors again.' "

Mort waited and, as nothing else was forthcoming, he prodded, "And? Then?"

"Then? Nothing. I looked at him and sort of smiled and scurried in here. I probably ought to have kept walking."

"Like a bird dragging its wing, heading away from its nest?"

"It's not funny," she snapped.

"Does he know your name?"

Loud: "No!"

"Your husband's name?"

Louder: "No!"

"Do you have friends in common?"

Loudest: "Not that I know of!"

Very softly: "So you're safe."

Nina stared sullenly out the dirty window at the back of the brownstone on the street next to theirs. It occurred to her that she would have to get a window washer to come in before the actor returned. It is against the law in New York to wash your own windows, because doing so is dangerous.

"I *feel* threatened," she said fiercely.

Mort began to pace and replied coldly, "I can see that."

"You don't have to get angry."

"Now *you* decide when *I* may be angry?"

"It's scary, losing my anonymity."

"He doesn't know your name."

"I don't know *his* name," she corrected.

"But the famous Nina Lathrop is a household word?"

"It's *your wife* who's famous."

"In a few select circles. What about me? My photograph was in the papers when I came to Twickham."

"You don't *care,*" Nina almost screamed. "You wouldn't be fired."

"Shut up, Nina. If the neighbors hear this, you *will* lose your anonymity. Keep your voice down."

Nina adjusted her voice to make up in intensity what it lacked in decibels. "Peggy Vandercook has guessed about us, I can tell."

"She won't say anything."

"Don't be too sure. You act as if Kitty will stay with you, no matter what you do."

"I don't do anything awful to Kitty. This is the only time I've ever—" he struggled to say the stilted phrase, "been unfaithful. And she might very well leave me, if she finds out. But"—his voice hardened—"I don't care as much as you do, because you and I have different values." His back was to her as he said, "I care most about preserving my relationship with you. You care most about preserving your relationship with David."

Mort reached the far end of the room and leaned against the door frame. His face was very pale. "Realistically, that stranger does not menace you, but you've projected your own feelings of guilt and fear onto him. We do take risks, coming here, and to you that stranger embodies them. It's not worth it, really. If you can't stand the heat, get out of the bedroom."

Nina wanted to embrace him but was unable to move. They stared at one another. Tears ran down her face and she spoke quietly: *"I yelled at you."*

Her response puzzled Mort, as if she had broken into a foreign tongue.

Nina explained. "Never in all my life have I yelled at a man or fought back. I snipe, snap, sneer, and sulk. I don't stand up for myself. I've never dared. I never felt secure enough." She hesitated, embarrassed, but he was still wounded, so she brightened and added, "It's wonderful. To feel so close to you and respect you enough so that we fight and I fight back. Usually I mollify."

"Respect?" He sat down on the beige velveteen couch.

She went over to sit beside him and hit her shin on the chrome base of the coffee table. "Ouch! With other men, I've felt that if I let loose, I'd demolish them. There's something sort of patronizing in not fighting back."

"You're kidding yourself. 'Cowardly,' not 'patronizing,' is the word."

"The replies that sprang into my head were so devastating that I didn't dare use them."

"How potent you are, my dear."

"With you, I not only know you can take care of yourself, but I trust my feelings for you not to be destructive. I've been angry for a long time."

"Ancient anger."

"From childhood. Infancy. I don't know. I had a few years of analysis, and that helped me to analyze myself, but there's a lot I don't understand. I'm more compassionate, since you. I can usually recognize displaced anger and replace it."

"You were angry a few minutes ago."

"It wasn't surrogate: this situation is anxiety producing. And I didn't yell at you much. But it's a start." She smiled and shrugged.

He stroked her brown curls. "I get angry at myself for putting you in this situation."

"I never think of it that way. We're in this equally."

"I can't help it. I was raised that way. I want to lead you out of this wilderness. I'm the man."

"I've noticed."

"Shall we end our affair?"

"Do you want to?"

"If it's too strenuous for you . . ." He scowled and thought. "I still don't."

"I couldn't." She rested her hand on his thigh. His warmth rose through his grey flannel slacks. "Whom would I yell at?"

"The kids."

"Bullying makes me feel tacky. That kind of yelling is a symptom."

He flushed. "Of what?"

Her hand slipped up to his zipper and slid it down, then went to work on his belt buckle.

"Only of that?" he asked.

"With us, that is a symptom, too," she replied, unknotting his tie. "An outward and visible sign of an inward, invisible grace."

"Oh my God, not another Episcopalian!" Mort groaned. "Kitty is an Episcopalian."

# 11

⟡⟡⟡

# MEANWHILE . . .

KITTY answered the telephone wearing only her new mink coat. It was turned inside out, so that the fur was next to her skin. When she had worn the coat on the street, the fur caressing her neck made her wonder how that softness would feel on her body. This morning, before she dressed, she got the coat from the front hall closet and reversed it. As she slipped into it, the telephone rang. Kitty threw herself across her double bed and picked up the white receiver.

David Lathrop wanted to buy one of her paintings. He needed her advice about which one to choose. He had been struck especially by a landscape and had not been able to get it out of his mind, but he wanted her assurance that it was right for his office. She knew the work he meant: she had painted a nude woman lying on her side, then had worked that into a hilly country scene; as far as she knew, no one had detected the underpainting.

"The topography suggests a female form," said David.

"Ahhhh," said Kitty, delighted. "I'm glad you like that one. It's a favorite of mine." Touching her seductively, the mink fur was silken and supple, making her aware of the areas where her skin was most sensitive.

118

"Will you come to my office then? To see the space where I want your painting to hang?"

Kitty believed that people who buy art should please themselves, but she was intrigued by this man, so she agreed to meet him at noon on the following day.

She arrived at his office wearing a buttery yellow dress, a wool and rabbit-hair blend, with delicate lace collar and cuffs. She had not worn makeup in the country, but as a New Yorker, she developed cosmetic skills and her eyes were subtly enhanced in neutral shades. She approached her face as she did a canvas, drawing on it, drawing it on.

The offices of Burgess, Lathrop and Hoffman were in midtown, on Park Avenue. Their receptionist was decorative, a pretty young brunette with an air of rather more breeding than Kitty expected to find in such a career cul-de-sac, but then Kitty had not been in very many Manhattan offices. She concluded that the brunette had probably taken the tedious job in hopes of finding a husband among the men who passed her desk and abandoning it forever. Kitty sat in an armchair in the handsomely furnished room. The chocolate carpet was thick, the walls were papered in a subdued print, the lamps were substantial. She had barely flipped through the latest *Fortune* when a pleasant, efficient-looking woman, in her fifties, appeared in the doorway and asked Miss Myers to follow her. Kitty had given that name to the receptionist, feeling it inappropriate for Mrs. Hinks to be here.

Kitty was led by David's secretary down a long, carpeted corridor, with doors along the right side opening into lawyers' expansive offices and doors along the left side opening into windowless cubicles of supporting personnel. There was a large library on the left, also, with an oval conference table in the center and armchairs at one end. David's was a choice corner office, and Kitty was amused by how cleverly it was decorated. The mixture of antiques and classic twentieth-century furniture was calculated to win over as many visitors as possible.

David's face became younger when he saw her. He was suave in his expertly tailored, grey pinstripe suit, white shirt, and grey tie with white polka dots, yet when he looked at Kitty, an irresistible innocence emanated from him. They exchanged pleasantries, feeling slightly naughty, as if this were not the straightforward business appointment that it in fact was (why had they not mentioned it to their mates?).

"There, over the couch, I think," said David, indicating the wall above a seating arrangement opposite his large, uncluttered, contemporary desk.

"Your colors in this room are so . . ." She sought the tactful adjective.

"Noncommital?" he offered, not without humor.

Kitty glanced up at him analytically. "You can hang any of them here, really. The scale is good."

They stood side by side, gazing at the empty space. She smelled uncannily like a bouquet of roses, and David bridled his impulse to nuzzle her straight blonde hair. Kitty was wondering what she was doing here. Many of her paintings would be at home in David's office. He did not need to consult her, yet she sensed no ulterior motive, no (conscious) scheme to see her away from Mort and Nina.

"Have you ever bought a painting before?" she asked.

David looked sheepish. "I guess it's obvious that I haven't."

"I'm immensely flattered."

"Perhaps I should look once more. When I saw your show, I wasn't thinking in terms of buying."

"You really ought. You'll see the paintings quite differently."

"Are you free?" He consulted his watch. "Will you have lunch with me, and then we'll go to your gallery and make the final selection?"

"That sounds grand. Just let me call the woman who owns the gallery and tell her we're coming. May I use your phone?"

"Please."

David left her alone, perhaps to instruct his secretary to break a previous luncheon engagement. Kitty hoped so. She had been a wife for eighteen years, taken for granted for most of them, and the prospect of a man rearranging his schedule in order to be with her was a tonic, whatever his motive.

David returned and helped Kitty into her mink coat, complimenting her on its beauty.

"Mummy gave it to me for Christmas," she replied, aware that her parents' wealth (and by implication, her own) added to her desirability. She wanted to be as desirable as possible, not to any end but to feel momentarily, at least, a woman, with all the magic and promise that can imply, and not simply a female person.

As they walked down the long corridor, Kitty experienced the disparity in their sizes as emphasizing his masculinity and her femininity: beside him she was petite, exquisite and fragile, valuable. Standing in the rising elevator, she asked inanely if his offices had always been in this building, and he answered as if it were an intelligent inquiry. They got off the elevator on the top floor and entered a private dining room, where a worn, chubby woman with dyed black hair and dark red lipstick acknowledged David with a nod and checked him off in a big book on a stand in front of her; no interloper had a chance of getting past her into the inner sanctum.

Kitty's coat was taken from her, and she and David were

shown to a table by the window, with a spectacular view of lower
Manhattan. A small vase of purple and red anemones marked the
center of the white tablecloth; the silver plate was heavy. There
were many more men than women in the room, all dressed in
conservative suits and ties. Grey and balding pates predominated.
At the tables where there were both younger and older men, the
younger ones were inclined to defer. There was no one else like
Kitty here, only a few stout wives in good tweed suits or female
professionals and executives, also in expensive suits, some with
vests. Kitty, in her butter-soft dress, with her slight figure (she did
not own a brassiere) was a mystery woman. David must enjoy
appearing with her, looking (in this company) like a mistress,
while their business was entirely aboveboard. Perhaps the men
who spoke or nodded to David or glanced at him intermittently
conjectured that she was an heiress with complicated divorce
problems; she was, after all, wearing a wedding ring.

The waiter took their drink orders. They both asked for Kirs.
Rolls were placed on their butter plates; their water glasses were
filled. Service was prompt and unobtrusive. When Kitty dined out
with Mort, their bill was not charged to an expense account, and
the modest restaurant's employees were more offhanded. Kitty
thought, "The place smells of money and influence."

She commented on the view, and they picked out landmarks.
Kitty was afraid that they would not have enough to talk about
to get them through the meal. She was wrong. They were revved
up, and since their previous conversations had been *en passant,*
at social gatherings, every topic was fresh for them. They discussed their work, David being as curious about how she had
evolved as a painter as Kitty was about how he had gotten to his
legal pinnacle.

By the time they descended to the street and agreed to walk

to the gallery (David explaining that he had canceled his early afternoon appointments and so was not rushed), they were so comfortable together that Kitty felt a spark of guilt. She was as secure in the virtue of their mission, striding up sunny Park Avenue, as an aerialist wearing a harness, but that did not negate her exhilaration. People stared at them, seeming to ask, "Who are they? They must be Somebody." With David, Kitty felt more attractive than she did with Mort; David was more virile with her than with Nina. David climbed the steep stairs to the second-floor gallery behind Kitty, and she was sorry that her mink coat hid her cute derrière. "Tush, tush," she thought, smiling at her pun.

Irene Martell was in her office, at the back of her gallery, when her painter arrived, client in tow. Irene, in her seventies, had short-cropped white hair. She made up her face in shades of grey: charcoal eyebrow pencil and mascara, ashy outline around her eyes, no lipstick, and over it all, a light dusting of stark white face powder. A startling face. She greeted them in a throaty voice, sizing them up and concluding that they were lovers. The notion pleased her, and as they followed her, Kitty and David pretended not to perceive her misconception. Another painter's work hung in the gallery, and Kitty's canvases were in a back room, stacked in grey metal storage bins. Irene flicked on the lights and left the couple there.

David put on his glasses and looked through the paintings silently, carrying a few of them to the window and examining them in the daylight. Kitty leaned against the window frame, sunshine backlighting her blonde hair, and watched alternately him and customers in the restaurant below. Stragglers, seated beside the large windows overlooking the courtyard, were having drinks, coffee, or a late hamburger. Kitty had eaten there many times; it was an informal establishment, where it was possible to have a light lunch for under five dollars. Finally, David spoke.

"This series is very witty. You've taken traditionally female matters and turned them into abstractions."

"Those are my most recent paintings. It took awhile to get up enough nerve to call a pile of dirty laundry, 'Composition in Whites and Colors.' "

David chortled. "I suppose you do risk not being taken seriously."

"Irene says someday there will be a footnote in a graduate student's thesis about the influence of the television commercial in Catherine Myers's work."

"Your dishes drying in a drainer on the sink is appealing."

"The most colorful is the sewing box with rows of spools of thread. But none of those is right for your office."

David came to the window, holding the landscape-over-nude. "This is definitely the one I most want to live with."

"You were correct about the female form. I painted a woman underneath." Kitty traced the body with her index finger and looked up into his warm, dark eyes.

His expression immobilized her, her finger still an inch from the canvas. He was candidly admiring of her painting and of herself, recognizing the woman beneath the surface of each. Kitty felt as if she were unfurling, opening like a blossom in time-lapse photography.

"You smell like roses," he said, and moved away to another painting. "I'm not certain whether this is childrens' blocks or skyscrapers."

"You're not supposed to be certain. It's the Fifth Avenue skyline, from the perspective of my living room on Central Park West."

David studied the picture, then searched for and found the portrait of a woman.

"That's my older sister, Sarah. She lives in San Francisco."

"Does she recognize herself in this?"

"It's really a geometric study. She's all angles."

"It's lovely. Is she?"

"Very."

"Luckily for me, the paintings that have been playing in my mind are still here. You've sold several since I saw your show."

"You have a good memory."

He looked at a few more canvasses and said, "I'm ready to do business."

"Right this way, sir." Kitty led him to Irene's office.

When they were seated around the white Parsons table, which served as Irene's desk, David took out his pipe.

"Do you mind?" he asked.

"Not at all," Irene lied. "Have you made up your mind?"

"The hilly landscape, the portrait of Catherine's sister, and the Fifth Avenue skyline."

"It's among those three?" Kitty had expected him to choose the landscape decisively.

"He's buying all three," Irene explained.

"No!" protested Kitty. "He didn't mean that."

David turned to Kitty with sudden intensity. "I did mean that."

Kitty stared at him. She could not have said what passed between her and David in that look, but it sufficed. David took a business card from his wallet and handed it to Irene, who was consulting her list and reading off prices. When Irene and David had completed the business details, he asked about frames.

"Do you want me to recommend a framer?" asked Irene.

"I want Catherine to choose the frames."

Kitty said tentatively, "I'll help you."

"Not help me. Do it. You know how your canvasses ought to be displayed. The landscape is for my office, the cityscape is for the reception room, and we'll hang the portrait in the hallway outside my office."

"The frames have to be absolutely simple, but they should be pleasing to you."

Irene interrupted them, addressing David. "You want the paintings delivered to your office, after Catherine has arranged the framing."

"Exactly." He knocked out his pipe and put it in a pouch in his breast pocket.

"Catherine?"

"All right. It's a responsibility."

"So is owning your work," said David.

Kitty beamed.

Downstairs, Kitty and David stood in front of the gallery entrance and faced one another, ready to go their separate ways.

"This is a very exciting day for me," said Kitty.

"For me, too."

They were enmeshed in euphoria and optimism. David leaned over to kiss her goodbye, aiming for her right cheek. She, interpreting the gesture as general, rather than specific, tilted her head to offer him her left cheek. Their lips met unexpectedly and firmly, softness and warmth eradicating all other considerations. Their kiss was brief but so wholehearted that when they pulled apart, they both grinned.

"Hello," said David.

"Hello," said Kitty.

He walked down Madison Avenue toward his office, and she

headed for Central Park West and home. With David, Kitty felt integrated. Irene and her clients valued the painter, while Mort required the wife. David eased her conflict, allowing her to be her whole self, an artist and a woman.

# 12

## TWONESS

NINA was already lying in the big brass bed by the time Mort walked into the apartment. There had been a faculty meeting and disguising their relationship had left them wanting to fall into bed together. As soon as the work day ended, that is what they did. This was the lovers' first full evening for themselves. They had both made excuses at home; David was away on business, which made it simple for Nina.

When they arose from bed, Nina prepared a steak (asking self-consciously how Mort liked it, relieved when he answered medium rare). She had popped potatoes into the oven to bake before undressing and she now cleaned and steamed fresh green beans and tossed a green salad with tomatoes and raw mushrooms. Mort supplied a mellow Burgundy. During her lunch hour, Nina had purchased on sale (to keep at their place) a long velour gown, the color of the wine, which she was wearing. Mort had dressed again in slacks and shirt. They ate by candlelight.

"Did you know," Mort asked, watching the flickering flame, "that Kitty had lunch with David yesterday?"

Nina's lips parted and her eyes opened wider.

Mort glanced at her and continued. "You did not. Well, my pet, your husband decided to hang one of my wife's paintings in his office. He invited her to come down and see the space, so that she could help him to choose. After he had—" Mort gave the phrase suggestive overtones: "shown her his walls, he took her to lunch."

"Where?" was all Nina managed.

"Some private club full of Establishment Mukdemuks."

"You're Establishment."

"My power is in molding the future. These blokes hold the reins of the present. We all know that governments no longer run countries. International corporations and the lawyers and bankers affiliated with them do. Kitty was quite undone. She said the pure power and influence in that room was palpable."

"Palpable?"

"Kitty talks that way." Mort sliced his steak with more energy than its tenderness required. "I'm told that David's office is enormous, furnished with fine antiques, and his suit was perfectly cut from expensive fabric, too."

"David just spent several thousand dollars at the tailor's. His firm has a new client, a communications conglomerate, and we're going to be filthy rich."

Mort flinched.

Nina amended. "David will be rich."

"How nice for you."

"Damn it, Mort, you know I don't care about that."

"Kitty does. She was intoxicated and restless last night. She'd had a taste of how life is meant to be."

"That's how I feel with you. But you seem kind of hurt by this."

Mort looked at her directly, his voltage on high, and said, "It's easier to run off with another man's wife than to watch him court yours."

"He's not 'courting' her. That's how he is with women. And he does admire her work."

"Wait. You haven't heard it all. David canceled his early afternoon appointments, and they went to Kitty's gallery, where he purchased not one, but three of her paintings. He's leaving the framing to Kitty. His office will pay for whatever she chooses. She has *carte blanche.*"

"I'm dumbfounded. Kitty told you all this?"

"With stars in her eyes."

"I wonder why David didn't tell me?"

"Think about it."

"Maybe he suspects you and me and wants to see if I find out. I'll have to watch it, so I don't let on I know."

"Kitty was too high to conceal her jubilation."

"Drunk?"

"More significant. Happy. High on happiness. They'd had wine, of course, and she doesn't ordinarily drink at lunch, but she's too smart to get tipsy with a client. She's not a drinker, anyway. Never before has she sold three paintings to a single client."

"Rich, influential people will see her work in David's office and perhaps become her clients as well?"

"She mentioned that."

"Yet you sense more than professional triumph? She's turned on by power and affluence?"

Mort's eyes filled with an appreciation of the intricacies of their situation.

"It is delicious," Nina said for them both.

"So is this salad." He chewed and swallowed. "You see, Kitty's parents are wealthy and she was raised taking that for granted, but she lived in a suburb of Boston, where money and privilege are restrained by breeding and taste. In New York it's all so blatant and, with all due respect to David, vulgar. Not that he is, but the overtness."

"Here people flaunt it. Jewels, furs, limousines, expensive restaurants, luxury apartments, travel, private clubs, clothes. David and I have had some incredible evenings lately, since we've gotten involved with these media types."

"The communications conglomerate? You never mentioned it."

"I try to forget. All that makes me terribly uncomfortable: rich French food, champagne, caviar, chauffeur-driven cars. Our entire life-style is changing and for the worse, as far as I'm concerned. For David to maintain us at that level means we never see each other, never talk. We're business partners in raising kids and furthering his career. Going up in society is a comedown. Our time alone together, which is what I care about with a man, is nothing. If it weren't for you, I'd be more isolated than when I was a divorcée."

"Glad to be of service. Kitty loves all that glitter. She's become more worldly since we moved here. In the country she was content. Always edgy and withdrawn before starting a new painting and distracted while working on it, but not covetous. Living in Manhattan on the relatively modest pay of a headmaster is forcing her to face the fact that people our age can and do have the sorts of perquisites you've been describing, in their own right, not as their parents' children, and that they're flourishing."

"But they sacrifice their intimate private lives."

"She saves all that for her work. She says I'm prying when I try to talk to her intimately, or else she doesn't hear what I'm telling her. Her soul is in her painting. Our girls are old enough so they don't require constant mothering. New York in general and David in particular have introduced Kitty to the high life at a time—she's forty-two . . ."

"David is thirty-nine."

"She's ready for a change."

"I can't believe one lunch did all that!"

"She was primed by renewing old school and college friendships, since we moved here, with women whose husbands are as successful as yours."

Nina held her long-stemmed glass so that the candlelight gleamed through the wine. "David says I have to have a new fur coat."

"Grand."

"I don't want another fur. He says Canadian lynx or a great-looking fox, but preferably mink."

"You prefer your old raccoon?"

"I'm to keep that for schlepping around the neighborhood, getting to school and back. The new coat is for our new social life. But I'm not a glamour girl. Kitty is."

"These days."

"My boys read *Ranger Rick,* a wildlife magazine. Rick is a raccoon. Greg and Zach cried when they realized my coat is raccoon."

"What did you do?"

"Said I won't deny my primitive nature. Predator and prey are the roles living things play. Raccoons kill fish and eat them. We all have to eat and keep warm. Wool coats never kept me warm. Vegetarians claim plants don't suffer from being killed and eaten, but now that's being questioned. People who don't wear fur and allege moral superiority because of it are hypocrites, unless they wear vinyl instead of leather and eat only unfertilized eggs, nuts, and milk."

"You're missing the point. Wild animals trapped for coats die horribly. Ranch minks are raised for coats and are humanely killed."

"I do not want a second fur coat, and I'm not a mink lady."

"Kitty's mother had her old mink coat, which is in beautiful condition, relined and gave it to Kitty for Christmas. Her mother considers living as a headmaster's wife hardship duty and tries to soften it for Kitty."

"Kitty loved the coat?"

"It made her Christmas."

Nina's eyes narrowed. "She probably wore it to lunch with David."

"Doubtless."

"That's why he announced last night that I have to buy a mink! The bastard."

Mort laughed and Nina reluctantly joined him.

She said, "David and Kitty are both star types."

"For what it's worth." Mort pushed his brown-specked stoneware plate aside and leaned back in his chair, drinking his wine. "David must know all about your 'primitive nature.' "

She faced him candidly. "Not as much as you do. David's and my sexual activity is much more, well, limited in scope, than yours and mine." The wine helped her to ask, "Why? Are you the same in bed with Kitty as with me?"

"Not at all. She saves her experimentation for her canvasses."

"David would be shocked by what we do."

"Kitty, too."

Nina frowned. "Do you think we're kinky?"

"Don't label us. If I could choose my sexual nature, or my partner's, I'd no more choose to need all the kinds of role playing and exchanging we pursue than you would choose, if you could, to eat animals and plants. Our sex life is like your fur coat—an acknowledgment of who we are, without censorship."

"I don't feel kinky."

"We're certainly not bizarre. What bothers you?"

"Like the time you opened my blouse and my breasts were bare and my excitement showed but you were dressed, still in your jacket and shirt. It really turned me on."

"Me, too."

"But your excitement was concealed beneath your clothes. Don't you see? That put me in an inferior position."

"And? Go ahead. Say it."

"Degrading."

Mort refilled their wine glasses, listening to her attentively. It was a luxury to have the time to linger at the table.

She said, "When I undressed you and, um, did everything, and . . ."

"I sat back and abandoned myself to your fantastic talent in that department."

"You were totally passive."

"I'd been making decisions, plotting strategies, and twisting arms all week at Twickham."

"You needed to be passive and rest, while I was aggressive."

"You experienced that as degrading for me?"

"David (and Kitty?) would think so."

"You must have done that to David. You're much too skilled to be learning on the job."

"Only as a condiment. Not as a one-dish meal."

"I see."

"I'm not criticizing or complaining. I love everything we do. I've never been so sexually alive and free. But I worry about whether being uninhibited is unhealthy, when it leads where it leads us."

"Oh, my darling, you must know, living in New York, that it doesn't lead us very far."

"I suppose. My sexual fantasies make me sad: I adore submission, being overcome—not by some uncouth rapist but by high-spirited, raunchy types; I have voyeuristic fantasies, slave fantasies."

"What kind would you like to have?"

"I wish love and tenderness were enough by themselves. I'd like to be totally turned on by making love in the missionary position in the dark with someone I love passionately."

"You are."

"Touché."

"But?"

"Not all the time."

"It doesn't trouble me that I can be passive or aggressive, the lover or beloved. I'm happy to come at the same time you do, with our eyes wide open, or to come alone, with my eyes closed, to watch you or to concentrate on other senses. Our moods change. That's why we keep needing each other."

"Partly. There's more."

"I love you so much that I'm happy to do anything that thrills and satisfies you, without judging it. You are who you are and you need what you need."

"Even if I wanted you to hurt me?"

"Pathology? Do you?"

"No!"

"I've never loved and trusted anyone except you enough to reveal my sexual nature as I've done here." He looked around the small living room. "And in the next room."

"And in the tub."

He grinned.

"With you," she said, "I feel as if I'm living my real life. The rest of the time, I feel as if I'm traveling incognito."

"You give me to myself, too."

# 13

✕◇✕◇✕

## FOLLOW THROUGH

KITTY chose three wooden frames: natural and veneers of gold and of silver. It was her idea that all David's paintings ought to have the same kind of frame, but she remained unwilling to make the final selection. She telephoned him and invited him to meet her at the frame shop. He accepted with alacrity. It was not, she told herself, that she wanted to see him again: that she was frequently visited by so sharp a memory of their kiss that her lips burned had nothing to do with this professional transaction. They were adults. Life in New York was more complex (and more interesting) than life in rural Massachusetts had been. This adventure was not without precedent in her daydreams, as she had organized the move to Gotham. An extramarital kiss was an event that a New England headmaster's wife might fuss about, but surely a New York woman took it in stride. Kitty was determined not to be provincial.

David framed her work in gold.

"Shall we walk?" he asked tentatively, their task done. "It's another lovely day."

"Fine," she replied brightly, putting him at ease. Beneath his show of confidence, she sensed the threat of desolation; he wanted her to help him avoid facing it.

He steered her out the door, his hand on her waist. His touch tamed her. The independence and assertiveness she evinced in regard to her work faded as she strolled with David, giving in to the luxury of being taken care of. He understood that it was he who effected this transformation, and he relaxed in the atmosphere of trust and well-being. Kitty's friendliness dissipated the chill he felt from living with Nina. His wife's cool contempt had of late been replaced by a polite boredom that she did not conceal as well as she thought. Kitty inferred a rejecting wife.

Ten blocks later David said, "There's an acceptable French restaurant around the corner. Shall we see if they can take us?"

Kitty hesitated only an instant. She smiled up at him and nodded. His hand went to her waist again and she felt naked beneath her fur coat.

When Kitty saw where David was taking her, her pulse quickened. It was one of those celebrated French restaurants where the status-conscious gather. Inside, the woman in the coat-check room greeted David by name. A man dressed in black tie came to him from the dining room.

"François, I didn't make a reservation," David said. "Can you take us?"

"Mr. Lathrop, let me see what we can do."

François surveyed the dining room, which was only half full, and indicated a table in the center. "I can seat you there."

Kitty was relieved, but David frowned and said, "Thank you, but I think not," turning to leave.

"Mr. Lathrop, one moment, please."

François went into the dining room and spoke confidentially to three middle-aged, slightly *déclassé* businessmen, sitting in a banquette, drinking what looked like martinis, and perusing menus. The three men stood up and moved to the table in the center of the room.

"I can't believe François is doing that," said David.

"Do you eat here a lot?"

"Once or twice a week, but my secretary makes reservations. He's moving those men."

Kitty tried to look blasé, but she was relishing every detail. François oversaw the changing of place settings and ushered David and Kitty to the banquette. David thanked him graciously.

"I can't believe he did that," David repeated.

"You wouldn't have moved?"

"Never."

"You're obviously more important than they are," said Kitty, removing the gracefully folded, heavy white napkin from her gold-rimmed service plate and laying it across her lap. "Are all the empty tables reserved?"

There were no little Reserved signs marring the tables' symmetry.

"Presumably."

They ordered Kirs, but David decided that they would not look at the menu yet. Seated on the beige plush banquette, beneath a mural of the Loire Valley, reflected in a mirror on the opposite wall, they once again found themselves talking easily and personally. Kitty had forgotten how absorbing it is to share life stories, not having had the opportunity for years. Neither she nor David was particularly introspective, so they reminisced without analytical digressions.

By the time the dessert cart was rolled up to their table, David saw not only the winding trail through a New England landscape that had pointed Kitty in his direction, but the colors and shapes of her daughters' young destinies. Gillian, active in

Twickham's film club, was going to be a filmmaker. Tessa was gloating in the confirmation of her womanliness, which a tardy menarche had this very week bestowed. Kitty discerned that David's drive and determination had sprouted while he was growing up in Manhattan, with parents who both worked full-time, his father as a lawyer, too, and his mother as a publicist for charitable organizations. An only child, David was still his ambitious parents' best hope for immortality, as they pursued retirement in Florida. David was trying to raise his own sons with the freedom and affection he had wanted and not received.

Kitty avoided the reflection of herself and David in the mirrored wall, but she kept glimpsing accidentally the good-looking couple so absorbed in their conversation that they could not possibly be married to one another. When David decreed that they should order, they both selected artichoke vinaigrette to begin. They scraped the soft grey-green flesh with their teeth, David arranging his spent leaves in a neat row around his plate, Kitty constructing a design with her leaves.

As an entrée, David had grilled sole, because he had learned that lunching as he did almost daily in expensive restaurants, he must avoid rich sauces and marbled meats. Kitty, who usually grabbed an apple and a hunk of cheese at noon, shunned the tyranny of calories and indulged in a truffled filet of beef *en croûte*, discovering *foie gras* in the wine sauce.

David ordered knowledgably from the wine steward: a half bottle of white for himself and a half bottle of red for her. Kitty liked his choice so much that she had two glasses. This meal with David was abundant in pleasures, and she relinquished her customary restraints without regret. The room had filled with people who looked as if their demanding standards for quality and stimulation were ordinarily almost attained. They were privileged, and they expected to remain so, or at least that is how Kitty saw them.

For dessert David ordered champagne to accompany the chocolate mousse. Although Kitty was too proud to admit that her daily life had none of the bubble and shine that evidently came naturally to David's, he got that message. The presence of a woman who appreciated what he had to offer, rather than sneering as Nina did, obviously liberated him. As the champagne was being poured into their glasses, he pressed his thigh against Kitty's. Her eyes widened, but she did not move her leg. They sipped *café filtre,* and David's hand (under cover of the white tablecloth) moved lightly to her lap. She laid her hand on top of his. Their conversation became stiff and empty. She wondered if he neglected to smoke his pipe because he expected to kiss her and did not wish to taste of tobacco. She marveled that she made this man happy, rather than simply content, as she did Mort.

David signed the bill for the meal, and they left the dining room. He held her coat and whispered into her ear, "There's a hotel across the street."

Kitty did not look at him. "All right," she said and marched out the door. He caught up with her on the sidewalk and led her through the midblock traffic into the hotel lobby.

"Go into the powder room or browse through the magazines in the drugstore," instructed David. "I'll check in. In ten minutes, you go to the house phone and ask what my room number is. Meet me upstairs."

Had he done this habitually? It did not matter. Kitty was not eager to be seen here with him by anyone she knew, so she appreciated his plan. As she wandered numbly around the drugstore, she remembered that Mort, not she, was sterile. Was David assuming that she was on the pill? There was no way to get her diaphragm. She had bought a new one when she heard that she was moving to New York, because she was unwilling to be totally dependent on Mort and his vasectomy. He had his own protection, and she was entitled to hers. Now, when she needed it, the diaphragm sat in pristine aloofness in a drawer at home.

Kitty sauntered up to the counter and said casually to the clerk, "Your smallest box of Trojans, please," praying inwardly that he not ask, "Large, medium, or small?"

She had never previously purchased condoms and had no inkling of what impossible choices she might be expected to make about style, size, and (judging by the vibrators in the display case) perhaps even color. The clerk seemed no more eager to discuss the subject than she, and he bagged and rang up a box for her without comment. She paid and retreated to the row of house phones in the hotel lobby.

David's voice was mellow and seductive. She hurried to the elevator, got off at the third floor, and followed an arrow to locate his room. He had removed his jacket and tie and partially unbuttoned the top of his shirt; dark hairs curled in the white V. He hung up her coat and unsmilingly enfolded her in his arms. His bulk and assurance thrilled her so much that her knees buckled. David and Kitty fell together onto the bed. He had already pulled back the spread. He undressed her slowly, looking at and touching her with more sweetness than she had guessed he had salvaged from his youth. His eyes and fingers covered every new area bared. She unbuttoned all his buttons and unzipped his zipper.

The sight of David's erection jolted Kitty. She looked away, neutralized with self-consciousness. Mort was the only man she had ever known in bed. David's experience was both more extensive and more recently extensive than hers (assuming that Nina was not his only sexual partner). He might find her inadequate, ignorant and gauche, in comparison with other women. David, gazing at her face, curved over her and kissed her, reviving her desire. She reached between his legs and was stunned by the unfamiliarity and throbbing insistence she felt there. In a primitive regression to phallic worship, she was his: not body and soul, but body alone, for her soul had been shocked into silence.

Kitty's body took over, as if it had been waiting for David's weight and lust, for the erotic thrill of the fragile-powerful handful she was stroking with mindless abandon. Kitty melted into awe beneath David's thrust. Streaming (as in a film she had seen, run in reverse, of an active volcano), churning hot toward the summit's brilliant convulsions. David did not use her Trojans. He came prepared. Their juices mingled, and their scent permeated the air. She loved that smell. David collapsed into the pillows, his hairy hand resting on her flat belly. She stared at the stained white ceiling and cherished the sensation of total relaxation and physical peace.

They showered separately, still not talking.

"May I call you at home?" asked David, as he carefully knotted his navy and white striped tie.

"Do." She let her ivory embroidered chemise fall over her head.

He kissed her moistly. "I will."

Their restrained smiles conveyed that more had happened than they had meant to happen, that they had touched feelings they had thought lost and gone, that they liked who they were at this moment more than they had liked themselves for a long time.

David left Kitty to finish dressing and to leave, after he was out of sight. She looked around the room. It was furnished in copies of French antiques. Without David it became impersonal and lonely. She got out fast.

Walking home along Central Park West, Kitty admitted that she had been restlessly ready for an affair. Mort's best energies and most of his time were spent away from her and their daughters these days. He was subtly hostile to her art. His vasectomy symbolized for her his lack of awareness of her as an independent person. He was not the sort of man who had that particular surgery because he was promiscuous, but the implication was that as long as he was safe from conception, so was she. Perhaps unfairly, she resented that.

David proved to her that the fine wrinkles at the corners of her eyes and mouth, the silver threads among the gold (they were few but not, to her, poetic), the arrival of the twentieth reunion announcement from her college, that none of these signs exiled her from the joys of passion. David had demonstrated that her failure to attract Mort in recent months was Mort's problem, not hers. But had this afternoon been a one-time thing? David's gentleness and her own responsiveness were perplexing. If she were being drawn into a romantic interlude, let it be.

The park looked barren and littered. Kitty recalled her walks in the unspoiled fields and hills around her former home. Here, people used the land and one another much harder. What did David want from her? Not devotion but something more atavistic. Not sex alone (he could have that with dozens of willing women) but sex with someone who admired him as Kitty did and whom he admired, so that her admiration was worth having, when he returned from the hunt with a buck. And most surprising, someone with whom he need not be tough. She smiled wryly at the mirrored box in which they found themselves.

Kitty felt loved for her wifely and motherly talents, but sexually, her husband had grown prematurely old. This was the only explanation she could devise for the dwindling of his sexual appetite since the beginning of the year, and for what Kitty viewed as his self-imposed starvation diet. She wanted to be wanted. She wanted to want. She had her work, her daughters, her position as headmaster's wife. What she had lacked, she now also had: a lover.

# 14

# EXCURSION

RESTLESS for space and freedom, Nina and Mort plotted a Saturday at the shore, having discovered that they shared a love of winter beaches. A simple outing it was not. Nina, walking from her home to the Seventy-second Street subway station, reviewed details. She had told David that today she was having lunch at Peggy's apartment in Brooklyn Heights and that they were then going to a matinée at the Brooklyn Academy. Nina had not related this scheme to Peggy, calculating that David was unlikely to telephone her at her friend's and that if he did, Peggy would instinctively protect her. Nina was to wait on the esplanade in Brooklyn Heights for Mort, who would park his car nearby. A rented car. He wanted to avoid his own car's being recognized. One day in the faculty lounge, Peggy had unwittingly provided Nina with a critique of the play, which she had seen and which they were allegedly attending together. Nina made notes afterwards and was prepared to give David realistic details.

Mort was to tell Kitty that he was going to visit the Brooklyn Museum. She had already been there and was urging him to go. He chose a Saturday when she had promised to take Gillian and Tessa shopping and was unable to accompany him. Earlier in the week, he made a quick trip to the museum and walked through

146

swiftly, picking up a catalogue and formulating a few aesthetic judgments to lend his story authenticity. Kitty thought that Mort was going to the museum by subway, but he left the subway in a neighborhood where he expected not to be known and where he had reserved a car at a rental agency.

Nina and Mort's Saturday was cold but sunny. Nina dressed privately, so that David would not ask why she wore thermal underwear beneath her brown wool slacks and blue Shetland cardigan. Her tan leather boots kept her feet warm as she walked down Broadway. She was looking at the sidewalk, thinking, when she heard a splatting noise: a truck had backfired and the startled pigeons, gathered on the triangular plot where Broadway angles across Amsterdam Avenue, were taking flight, their wings sounding like rain on the pavement.

She crossed Seventy-second Street and descended into the subway. Underground, people looked their worst—sallow, poor, and deranged, even people who looked normal and reasonably prosperous on the street. Waiting for her train, Nina paced the platform, remembering Peggy's story about the day that a maniac lurched into the subway car in which she was seated, brandishing an ax. Peggy had thought, "The kind of day I've had, he'll head straight for me," and he did.

Standing over her, his eyes wild, his feet spread apart for balance, he lowered the ax, with both hands, toward Peggy's skull. She was sitting by the door, beneath the cage that housed the sign on which the train's destination was printed. The ax caught on the metal bars protecting that sign. With felicitous timing, the subway pulled into a station and shrilled to a stop, the man stumbled off, the doors closed behind him, and Peggy lived to tell the tale, which did not make the newspapers.

Nina's train rumbled to a standstill, and she boarded with

other people who had collected on the dimly lit platform. She found a seat and looked around her. A man across and down the aisle from her was staring and smiling at her. She lowered her eyes, and he pulled open his fly and flashed. A seasoned New Yorker, she showed none of what she felt: shock, irritation, amusement, interest, revulsion, and pity. She looked out the window into the dark tunnel, thinking, "He isn't circumcised. I've never seen an uncircumcised one before." She wanted to peer at him, to study his foreskin, but she did not. The man did not follow her when she changed trains.

Several trains went by before hers came along. Their exteriors were covered in bold graffiti, and she puzzled over why some of her fellow-citizens objected to them. She found them cheerful and decorative. She was, nonetheless, relieved to climb into the sunshine in Brooklyn and find her way to the esplanade. She scrutinized the crowd, not wanting to see anyone she knew. Strangers. All strangers. Perfect. She went to the railing and gazed across the East River at the beautiful Manhattan skyline.

"Good morning," said Mort's voice behind her.

She whirled around. "Fancy meeting you here."

He told her where the rented car was parked ("An orange Pinto, unfortunately") and they walked to it along different routes. They did not dare to kiss in the car, in case an acquaintance passed by.

"Guilt makes you crazy," observed Mort, nosing the car into the traffic.

Nina told him about the flasher and about the ax-man.

"Isn't that a Beatles' song? 'The Ax-Man'?"

"Ouuu, bad."

"You'd better stay off subways. Take busses."

"Thanks."

They did not talk very much. It seemed odd to be in a car together, as if they were married or dating, both familiar and strange. The previous summer, Mort had driven his family to the beach a few times, but he was hazy about directions. He had put a map in the glove compartment and asked Nina to navigate.

"Oh, lord," she thought, "just like a wife."

They found the beach without once getting lost. In the parking lot there were three other cars, all empty. Finally Nina and Mort kissed.

"Us, necking in a parking lot," said Mort incredulously.

They locked the car and followed the sidewalk through dry sea grass to the sand. The wind was chilly, and Nina pulled up the collar of her pea jacket and put on her beret. Mort wore a blue goose-down ski jacket, jeans, and leather boots. They trudged along the pebbled shore, close to the slate-grey water. The tide was going out, depositing debris as it went. The air was salty.

"This morning I got a letter from my mother in Sewickley," said Nina, taking Mort's arm. "I was reading along, and I thought I'd flipped out. She's saying that my father has discovered a pair of thirteen-hundred-dollar sneakers, which he wants desperately and which he'll probably end up buying."

"Thirteen-hundred-dollar *sneakers?*"

"That's what I thought. I mean, where would he *wear* them? I was trying to picture what you could *do* to sneakers, even hand-crafted and gilded ones, to make them worth thirteen hundred dollars, and then I was trying to figure out why my father, who doesn't even jog or anything (and you don't wear sneakers to play golf, do you?) would yearn for such fancy footwear." Nina started to laugh. "Then my mother mentioned something about an amplifier, and I realized I was so rattled about meeting you today that I'd misread 'speakers' as 'sneakers.' "

Mort laughed, too. "Speaking of jogging, shall we?"

They took off at an easy pace. Except for two black men, walking a black and white spotted dog, they had this stretch of beach to themselves. As they passed, one man was saying to the other, "So she said, 'I did everything I could to save my marriage.' And do you know what she was wearing? Her wedding gown!"

"What can they be discussing?" asked Nina.

"I can't imagine."

When they were tired, they strolled off the sand and into a children's playground. Slides, swings, seesaws and a junglegym were surrounded by a chain-link fence with a broken gate hanging on one hinge. They sat on adjacent swings, pushing occasionally with their feet, to achieve gentle, irregular motion, without pumping.

"Did you hear what happened to Linda Babcock?" asked Mort.

"Neither of my classes has art on Fridays, and she wasn't in the lounge."

"She left early. Her mother and her psychoanalyst both died, her shrink on Thursday and her mother yesterday."

"Poor dear! She must be a basket case."

"When she came to my office, to explain why she was leaving, she seemed emotionally paralyzed."

"Either she'll be wiped out by this, or she'll be free. Woody Allen says he's not afraid of his own death, he just doesn't want to be there when it happens."

"Free?"

"Freeee . . ." chimed Nina, leaving her swing and running across the hard dirt to mount the ladder of the slide. "Freeee . . ." she sang, spreading her arms wide and sliding down.

Mort ran after her and she bolted to the junglegym. He

pursued her to the top of the frigid bars. She kept climbing, beyond his reach, taunting him playfully, then jumping to earth and dashing out the gate. He chased her onto the beach, where he caught her at water's edge and kissed her. His hand moved inside her pea jacket and her cardigan.

"Definitely a breast man," thought Nina, appreciatively. David was not.

She sighed with contentment. "It's lovely being outdoors with you, in the sun and air."

Mort squatted down and picked up two large broken clam shells, handing one to her and digging with the other. She squatted beside him, and they piled and molded wet sand into a baroque castle, surrounded by a moat, which they decorated with bits of shell, sea glass, twigs, and seaweed. Nina found a skate's egg purse and positioned it as a drawbridge. Mort stuck a seagull's feather in the central tower.

"Did you know that homosexual male pouter pigeons build the most highly decorated nests in pouter pigeondom?" asked Mort.

"Not actually."

"In heterosexual pairs, egg-laying cuts off nest-building activity, but there's nothing to stop all-male pairs, so they go on decorating, making their nests' inside's and outside's more and more beautiful."

"Sort of like people."

Nina's legs were cramping, and she stood up.

"Pam thinks that women can't be both lovers and mothers," she said, "And that childless women have the sexiest, most intimate and romantic relationships with men."

"Pam must be childless."

"Natch."

"You're living proof that she's wrong."

He took Nina's hand, and they started to walk again. Ahead of them, seagulls were screeching over a tasty morsel.

"Does Pam like to put you down?"

"She's nifty. She does yoga and went through an Eastern religion phase and all that. She still meditates daily and says it works for her. She also says that acquisitiveness is the real key to fulfillment and that she's gotten *beyond* looking inside herself for fulfillment; now she looks inside boutiques."

Mort smiled. "My brother, Terrence, and his wife were in town last weekend."

"I know."

"He told me he'd been to a convention in Chicago and he was furious that the room his firm reserved for him was tiny, with no real bed, only a couch that pulled out. The bath had a shower but no tub. He's accustomed to a suite. After he'd thought about it, he began to sweat. He decided that it was the old pink slip, and he was about to be fired."

"How dreadful." Nina stared out to sea, where a freighter glided slowly along the horizon.

"On the last day of the convention, Terry was searching for a missing shirt and opened a door he hadn't touched before. Behold! A living room, complete with flowers, well-stocked bar, and impressive view. Beyond that, a bedroom with twin beds. Then a dressing room and bathroom, featuring not only a huge tub but a bidet and a telephone. Biggest suite his firm had ever taken for him, and he'd only occupied the sitting room."

"You're making that up."

"You haven't met Terry."

"I'm getting cold."

"Shall we head back?"

"I know people here who've taken it."

"Would you?"

"It's not my sort of thing."

"Me neither."

Mort paid their check and they headed back to Manhattan, sad to see their day end but determined not to arrive home so late that they kindled suspicion.

"I wish we had the evening, too," said Nina, as they entered the Midtown Tunnel under the East River.

"In bed."

"In bed."

"Monday?"

"Monday."

He dropped her off at First Avenue and Forty-second Street, chancing a quick kiss. She took a bus across town and up Broadway, getting off a block and a half from her apartment.

The day had whetted their appetites for space and freedom.

They turned toward the exit to the parking lot.

"Was that story a non sequitur?" asked Nina.

Mort considered before answering. "Pam's insecurity at not having children is as irrational as Terry's about his worth his company. People have attacks of self-doubt."

"Speaking of absurdity, did you hear that when Nixon s copies of his Watergate book at two hundred and fifty doll each, as being personally autographed, they were signed by automatic electric pen?"

"Is that true?"

"I don't know."

They left the sand. The macadam sidewalk was hard benea their feet.

"Are you hungry?" asked Mort.

"Ravenous."

They arrived at the orange Pinto, got in, and drove towa the city, stopping at a roadside restaurant for fried clams. Happ to be in public together, as if they were a married couple, the spent half an hour over coffee.

"When Nicole was here," said Nina, "She told me that he current stepmother, Louise, is taking E.S.T."

"Your first husband's current wife."

"You've got it. She's taking E.S.T. in self-defense."

"Against what?"

"Not 'what.' 'Whom.' Nick took it and became impossible to live with. More impossible, I'd say. Louise broke her three best vases throwing them in frustration, because she could no longer win an argument with him, after his E.S.T. training. She told Nicole that she either had to take E.S.T., too, or give up gardening, because she wasn't going to have any vases left for her flowers, the way things were going."

# 15

#### ✦✦✦✦✦

# BONDING

WHEN Kitty's gold-framed paintings were delivered to David's office, he invited her to come in and supervise their hanging. The scene had overtones of domesticity, with David holding a painting at various levels against the wall, and Kitty telling him which was right. He marked the spot with a soft pencil, so a maintenance man could install a secure hook the next day. They repeated this process two times, finishing with the landscape above David's couch.

"Do we have the evening?" he asked.

"I told Mort I'm having dinner in SoHo with a friend."

"When does he expect you?"

Kitty hesitated, reluctant to disclose how devious she had become and how available, before confessing: "I said she and I are going on to a rap session with other women painters, so I might be late."

David encircled her with his arms, and they kissed.

"There's a screening I'm supposed to attend at eight. Want to come?" he asked.

"Won't there be people there who know Nina?"

"That crew is nothing if not discreet."

"Okay."

"Shall we eat afterwards, or are you famished?"

"Afterwards, yes."

"Then we can repair to the hotel during the interim?"

"I hoped we might."

As before, Kitty met David in the hotel room. Making love to repletion created other appetites. David ordered smoked salmon and white wine from room service.

"We can walk to the screening," he said when they had dressed and eaten. He drew on his pipe and watched her reaction.

"It's dark outside. Let's live dangerously," she said gamely.

They walked in a leisurely fashion to a large office building; beside the bank of elevators David told a grey-uniformed guard why they were there. They took an elevator to a reception room carpeted in dark red. A woman with a silk dahlia in her wavy brown hair checked David's name off on a list and handed him two sheets of white paper giving the film's cast, credits, and hype. David nodded and spoke to several of the two dozen or so men and women gathering to see the movie. Kitty overheard a man of about David's age say, as they passed, to the wifely-looking woman with him, "That's the lawyer I was telling you about."

Kitty wondered if she looked like wife, date, or colleague. Wives accompanying their husbands to business functions seem self-contained, while businesswomen's energies flow outward. Kitty had a flash memory of examining slides in botany class: wives are parameciums and female colleagues are amoebas. Career women change from amoebas to parameciums when they act as adjuncts to their own husbands' careers, although they push at the restraining membrane. Husbands escorting working wives seem to be protozoa out of water.

In the private screening room, David and Kitty slipped into aisle seats two-thirds of the way back. Kitty judged the room to be about one-quarter full. The deep red padded seats, which reclined slightly, were wider and more comfortable than commercial theatre seats, and the rows were farther apart to provide ample leg room. There were ashtrays on the backs of the seats, but David did not smoke his pipe.

The film was a supernatural thriller about a teenage boy who evokes a psychotic poltergeist. When David asked Kitty later, over supper, what she had thought of it, she replied, "Scary. Creepy. Well-enough acted. Utterly unbelievable."

"They'll line up for it in droves?"

"Probably. I've never seen this genre before."

"What did you think of the audience?"

"I barely met anyone."

"They have a look."

"Cool. Cold. Competent. Insecure. Driven."

"Bull's-eye."

"Do you like them?"

"Some of them."

The waiter served Kitty's linguine in white clam sauce and David's *saltimbocca alla romana*. They had salad next and then espresso. David had made reservations at *La Nouvelle Vague,* a popular discotheque, "just in case."

Kitty consulted her watch and intoned solemnly, "It's eleven o'clock. Do you know where your spouses are?"

David's smile pressed his question.

"I'd love to," she said. "I've read about the *Vague* but I've never been there. I guess we women are having a very heated and involved rap session tonight."

"I don't want you to get into trouble at home."

"Mort said he'd probably be asleep when I got back."

David paid the check, and Kitty drifted into contemplation

of why she was taking risks with a man she did not love. David stimulated and amused her. Being involved with him replaced familiar anxieties with new, more vivid ones. He distracted her, and she found herself in great need of distraction. When she let down her guard, he touched her too deeply for this kind of an affair, and she struggled to regain her distance.

Outside the restaurant David hailed a cab, and they drove through a shabby commercial section on the fringe of midtown and pulled up in front of an old warehouse, with velvet ropes marking its entrance and holding back a small knot of people. Kitty did not know if they were simply waiting for a glimpse of arriving celebrities or if they hoped to be admitted.

A young man in a Chesterfield coat, who had been barring the door, opened it for Kitty and David. Inside was a darkly mirrored lobby, with a dark carpet, on top of which was a long rubber mat, forming a protective pathway to the reservations desk (which looked as if it had once served in a small hotel). The young woman behind the desk spoke with an English accent. Her skin seemed transluscent. She affected a disdain calculated to turn on the sadomasochists who put their self-esteem on the line with the arbiters of admission into key watering places.

"We don't have your reservation," she told David.

"Sure you do," he said good-naturedly. "I can read upside down." He pointed to his name in her book.

"All right." She was satisfied that he played the game.

David checked their coats, and they went through double swinging doors into the entryway. There was a pool with a footbridge through a tunnel of water: an arch of clear plastic, approximately eight feet high at its apex, enclosed the bridge, and over this arch cascaded water, collecting in the pool below (before recirculating). Colored lights shone beneath the surface of the pool, set in a rock grotto, and baby spots played over the waterfall. Crossing the bridge, Kitty and David were surrounded by a rainbow of water. Kitty looked up, laughing with childlike delight. David kissed her spontaneously, and they were both embarrassed by the intrusion of genuinely innocent emotion.

In the enormous, rectangular inner room, each long side was banked by velvet couches rising from the central dance floor in tiers of watery colors. On the table in front of each couch a dim light glowed under a sea urchin shade. Just beyond the entrance, there was a bar built around a dancing fountain, which rose and fell in time to whatever record blasted out of the loudspeakers. The bar itself resembled a coral reef and the bar stools looked like fuscia jellyfish, with tentacles of silver link chains hanging from their bright seats. The barmen and waiters appeared to be barely of legal age and wore black bikini bathing suits and Greek sandals. Their trays were lucite set in black rubber, designed to look like giant diving masks. Kitty wondered if these young men waxed their chests, as all were hairless.

At the opposite end of the room was a huge screen on which played acquatic pictures. Sometimes giant waves broke over the dancers' heads, at other times, hallucinatory images ebbed and flowed in mind-leveling abstractions. Heavy pipes on the ceiling held spotlights, which transformed dancers into frenetic puppets on ribbons of light. David took Kitty's hand and led her up the stairway among tiers of couches until they found a vacant one. He removed his jacket and tie and rolled up the sleeves of his white shirt. Kitty peered through the shadows at the apparitions on neighboring couches, several of whom were in advanced stages of foreplay: men with women, men with men, but no women with women, as far as she could see.

"Do you want a drink?" asked David.

"I want to dance."

She tucked her purse under an overstuffed mauve pillow on their couch and they descended to the dance floor. Kitty caught the toe of her shoe and looked down. The wood parquet had been laid in squares, which were warping around the edges. She eased between dancers to a space on smooth flooring and David followed. They began slowly until the music and lights blew their circuits and they moved into frenzy. When strobes began blinking very quickly, Kitty felt disoriented by the illusion that the dancers became stationary. She danced wildly, radiance and rhythm dissolving her reality. The other dancers suggested, whenever the strobes flashed fast, frescoes of hell in musty Italian churches—beguiling creatures in outrageous poses.

It all dropped away from her: pain, responsibility, integrity, disappointment, loyalty, fear, mortality, time. She let them all go, gave them up gratefully, shaking them off with ferocity and style, sliding easily from barbarism to elegance to obscenity, from exaggeration to restraint, from big to small and expanding again, her glazed eyes staring into David's.

When they paused to rest, she said, "I'm going to the loo. I'd love a Perrier."

"I'll meet you at the sofa," he said.

The women's room was under one tier of couches, the men's room under the other. A striking blonde in white crêpe pajamas printed with delicate rosebuds was sitting on the dressing table top, in front of the mirror, talking to a redhead in a tan-fringed vest (only that, no shirt) and a thigh-length, fringed skirt. Kitty heard her say, "Most of the men here look like hairdressers."

The girl ahead of Kitty in line wore a white lace baby-doll nightgown over a flesh-colored leotard. A leonine black woman had transparent plastic tubes woven through her hair, like a futuristic crown. The jeans people were present, too, mingling with the funky costumes. Kitty went into a stall wearing a well-bred brown wool dress and emerged carrying it under her arm, clad only in her underwear and shoes. In anticipation of another bedroom scene with David, she had worn a new, ecru cotton camisole, trimmed with eyelet and blue ribbons; the matching half-slip fell in flounces to her knees. They reminded her of the underwear worn by girls in bordello scenes in Western movies. Now she evaluated herself in the mirror, to be sure that she looked more dressed than undressed.

David did not recognize her, mounting to their couch. He glanced at her impersonally, then stood automatically when she joined him.

She said, "Do you think my lingerie will pass?"

He kissed her. She stuck her dress under the pillows with her purse and drank her Perrier water thirstily. David's drink looked like Scotch. The air was sweet with marijuana. Kitty reached over and unbuttoned David's shirt half-way to his waist, so she could see his chest hairs. She took off one of her gold chains and fastened it around his neck. They both were able to live with the symbolic significance of the gesture, and so it marked a change in the status of their relationship.

"Shall we dance?" she said.

They danced and danced, Kitty discovering how liberating it is not to care. She felt both dead and more alive. Nothing mattered except giving in to the manipulative lights and music.

At one A.M., David took her home in a cab. They did not talk very much. After they had kissed goodbye, David said that he would call her soon, and she was confident that he would.

Upstairs, Kitty found that Mort was indeed already asleep.

She looked in on Gillian and Tessa, also sleeping deeply, and then she got ready for bed.

She slid under the covers beside her comatose husband, but she did not fall asleep right away. She was remembering Waltz Evening in Boston, more than twenty years earlier, and arriving there in her father's Bentley. The floating happiness, the elegance and romance, which had nothing to do, really, with how she felt about her partner when they were not on the dance floor. He placed his hand firmly on the middle of her back and whirled her off around the room until she was flying, safe in his sure arms, exhilarated that her feet and legs were moving in precise and tricky synchronization with his. Those years of dancing school (girls in velvet dresses and Mary Janes, boys in suits and ties, all in short white gloves) suddenly made wonderful sense. She was in love for the space of a waltz, whether gliding and swirling with her favorite beau or with her father's stodgy stockbroker.

Where had it all gone? No man had *led* her for such a long time. Today, a man *rested* his hand on her back when they danced traditionally. No more the authoritative grasp, the certain pressured guidance, the pleasure of executing, with sensational speed and grace, steps you had both mastered. Instead: drifting aimlessly in your partner's arms. Many of the men with whom she had taken to the floor for a recent fox trot must have been to dancing school, may have been excellent dancers in college, unhesitatingly sweeping their partners through perfectly timed patterns into heady liberation. When had they lost the knack—or the nerve?

Disco dancing is much more democratic, Kitty decided. No need for dancing school, just the will to give in to the beat and a willingness to see what happens. No need for white gloves to censor the fingers. Dancing without touching physically, screwing without touching emotionally. Kitty thought groggily, "One-night stands wear white gloves on their hearts."

As a woman who has known and enjoyed many men must long for the lost lover who most made her feel happy, Kitty longed to waltz. Not to abandon the hustle, but to have them both. From her perspective, waltzing was symbiotic, horizontal, formal, and optimistic, while hustling was self-reliant, vertical, improvisational, and disillusioned. One was a Bentley, the other a subway. Each had its place in her life and she did not want to eliminate either. A subway gets you there faster, but a Bentley makes you feel that you have arrived. And the destinations are different.

\*

David and Kitty saw one another two or three times a week. They lunched in chic restaurants, not likely to be frequented by anyone from Twickham but popular with celebrities. In the late afternoon, they met in cocktail bars where a pianist played schmaltzy mood music and the lights were dim. On occasional evenings they dined and danced, Kitty using the fictional rap session with fellow women artists as an excuse for Mort and feeling frivolous for doing so.

David entertained Kitty with the continuing saga of his work with colorful media folk. Kitty listened, comprehended, interpreted, inferred, and suggested. Her own work flagged, but she assumed that this was only a 'phase' in her life, a phase beyond which she did not attempt to peer. She joined an exercise class and was healthy and energetic.

They were prepared for a Twickham parent to turn up and recognize them at any time. They planned to say that Kitty was consulting David about legal problems arising from the sale of one of her paintings. To appear together openly, they decided, placed them above suspicion in most situations. Both of them might legitimately visit a friend or client in a respectable hotel, but only adultery would take either of them to a shabby one, so they stuck with class. Walking from restaurant or bar to hotel, however, they took the precaution of splitting up, meeting in what became 'their' room. The fake French furniture continued to offend Kitty, but she usually shut it out of her consciousness.

\*

"I signed the lease today," Kitty told David over shad roe one warmly dreamy April day.

"For a studio?"

"The one on Broadway."

"That's wonderful. You're sure it's safe to store your paintings there?"

He leaned back in the curved red banquette. This was their favorite restaurant, because its dark red walls and individual banquettes gave them a sense of being inconspicuous; no one sat within hearing distance. The fact that there were often famous people in the room also added to their own anonymity. When David's clients showed up, they were not a problem, because they expected him to be seen with beautiful women.

"I'm having an electric lock installed on the door," said Kitty. "No one can get in through the studio windows. The light is good. The light is terrific, after trying to paint in my apartment. And at last I have adequate storage space."

"You'll get more work done, now that's settled."

"That's what I want to talk to you about. Here. While you still have your clothes on."

David's mouth smiled but his eyes did not.

"I want to paint you."

"I'd be recognized."

"I don't want to paint your face."

His eyes clouded and he waited.

"I've never done male nudes, but your body is so . . . so . . . impressive that I want to paint you. Not pornography, *ça va sans dire.*"

"Have you painted female nudes?"

"Not since I was a student. There's the one you have in your office."

"With the hidden lady. You're asking my permission?"

Kitty picked up her salad fork and drew a pattern in the tablecloth by pressing down on the tines. "I want you to pose."

"While you sketch?"

"That would take more time than you have to give." Kitty was not able to ask what she had to ask.

"I don't know what you want from me," said David.

"I have a Polaroid camera in my purse."

"You want me to pose for *feelthy peekshurs!*"

Kitty laughed but said seriously, "This is very hard for me."

"Let's drop it."

"I can't. Your body haunts my vision."

Pause. "Wow." Pause. "Okay. I'll think about it."

David disappeared inside himself, and they finished their meal in silence, forgoing dessert.

In the hotel room, David sat on the edge of the bed and said, as he removed his shoes and socks, "Will you promise never to photograph my head?"

"Of course." She sat down beside him but did not undress.

"And to cut up and flush down the toilet each photo as soon

as it has served its purpose and always before you leave your studio. You won't leave them there, or in your purse, or anywhere?"

"I promise."

"I'm still thinking about it." He got up and laid his suit neatly over a chair. "Why don't you paint yourself?"

"I don't want to. Except, maybe, down there." She was embarrassed but refused to be shackled by her upbringing. David gave her the security she needed to grow. "You say I'm beautiful there, and do you realize that in the history of Western painting and sculpture, that area of the female has been so taboo that you hardly ever see it? There's a statue in the Rodin Museum in Paris. . . . Well, I'm tempted—" She broke off, shaking her head.

"Go on," he encouraged tenderly, standing over her.

"To use a mirror and try an abstract rendering, perhaps a male-female combination. Lovers. But I don't want them to be titillating."

"Or to violate the bounds of good taste," he teased.

"There's nothing wrong with good taste."

"I've never before seen myself as a sex object."

"Sex object!" she almost shrieked. "David Lathrop, that's not how I see you!"

"Shucks. I guess I'd better do something about that."

David and Kitty came to terms, and she began a series of nudes, mostly of a male but a few of a male and female together, faceless and compelling. Kitty felt that they required of her new courage. David was proud of them and of her, but Mort never got around to visiting her studio to see them. Irene proclaimed them her best work.

# 16

## DECISION

In April, Nina and Mort spent the night together.

Kitty had taken the girls to Massachusetts for the weekend to visit her parents. David was on the Coast on business. Nina announced that she was going to Gretchen's for dinner on Saturday night; at ten o'clock she telephoned Coral to say that she was having such a good time that she was staying over (to avoid taking a cab alone, late at night). This entailed confessing to Gretchen, so that if Coral telephoned her, in an emergency, Gretchen could relay the message to Nina.

As Mort and Nina sat on the couch, after clearing away their dinner dishes, she said, "It was hard telling Gretchen. I worry, anyway, about what my parents and friends would think, if they knew."

"You have a lover and a husband, an embarrassment of riches."

"She's glad for me but it hurt. She needs a man."

"Does she think you're insane to stray from so attractive and successful a husband?"

"Not at all. Her ex-husband was climbing the corporate ladder."

"She must resent your enjoying the rewards of David's ascent, without suffering the loneliness. I take care of that."

"Harsh."

"Accurate."

"She's too good a friend to resent me. She knows I don't enjoy the dual roles. Like Valentine's Day. It was no joke buying cards for both you and David. I went to two different stores, so the clerk wouldn't suspect."

"Paranoid."

'And then you gave me tulips, and I wondered what you gave Kitty."

"A chocolate 'K.' "

"With a card saying, 'Sweets to the sweet'?"

"Not exactly, sweetheart. Do you know the last word of that quote?"

"No."

" 'Farewell.' It's 'Sweets to the sweet: farewell!' "

Nina said nothing.

"I also sent my secretary, in the hospital, a flowering azalea."

"Because she had her baby on Valentine's Day. That was nice of you. The 'K' doesn't thrill me."

"It wasn't intended to." ·

"David's and my sex life isn't what it was."

"Neither is mine with Kitty."

"I can't tell if it's because of me, or if David has cooled, too."

"Kitty has always been a very private person."

Nina kissed him gently. "I'm sorry I've made you feel disloyal."

"I love you."

"It's confusing."

The week had been hectic, and they had not managed to see

very much of one another. Mort took Nina's hand and said, "You've become distracted lately."

"I oughtn't discuss this with you. It has nothing to do with you."

"Try me."

"David and I are looking at cooperative apartments on the East Side."

Mort was uncomprehending.

"David decided that, because of our glorious new position, we have to buy a fancy apartment over here. He knew I'd resist, so he did the ground work, without telling me."

Mort, no longer relaxed, listened at the alert.

"David came home about a week ago and said he'd found four apartments he thought were definite possibilities. I went to look at them with him. One was on Fifth Avenue and I could see your apartment building from it. I imagined you and me flashing messages across the park. Then I felt opportunistic for seeing my home with him in terms of you."

"Did you take an apartment?"

"I told David I can't get accustomed to the idea so fast, and I'm not wild about any of them, anyway. I need more time. I said we should keep looking."

They stared dumbly at one another.

Mort said, "The *truth* is what we don't want to talk about."

Moving required reaffirmation of Nina's commitment to David. She did not want to make it, did not know how to avoid it.

"Are they large apartments?" Mort asked, his voice tight.

"Larger than our present one and much grander."

"The timing is awkward."

"To understate."

They kissed, but their coming together had the frantic quality of an escape. Mort pulled free and said, "Let's dance."

"What?"

"Let's dance."

"Dance?"

He went to the phonograph and put on one of the actor's
records. Nina switched off the lights and slid into his arms. They
had never danced together before. They danced, barefoot on the
white shag rug, until they felt inseparable, and then they went to
bed.

This weekend was supposed to be their happiest time, but
it was shadowed by recognition that were Nina to move with
David, it marked the end of her and Mort's affair. It would
symbolize the permanence of of the Lathrop marriage. Moving
and decorating would consume Nina's spare time. The new apartment might conceivably be in the same neighborhood as the one
where she now lay in Mort's arms. It was a quandary.

Awakening together, naked in the soft April light, was not
the joy that they had anticipated. Anxiety put distance between
them. Lovemaking became an opiate.

The previous day, Nina had stopped at a bakery and bought
croissants. She carried them to bed on a tray, with coffee, hot
milk, butter, honey, and freshly squeezed orange juice. They sat
propped up and scattered crumbs on the actor's chic brown-
patterned sheets.

"When I was a teenager," said Nina, "I slept all morning on
weekends, but I can't do that anymore."

"You were retreating from all those problems you thought
you had: too tall, too smart, not beautiful enough."

"Not beautiful at all."

"Now you realize that your height, your brains, and your looks are assets."

"Sure, sure. And as a teenager in Michigan, you anaesthetized yourself, too, against the pain of feeling too short, too angry at your parents' midwestern conservatism, and what that did to your life, the irritation of having your younger brother be a jock, when you weren't."

Nina and Mort had exchanged autobiographies (as lovers will), stressing their inner lives. Unlike twenty-year-olds, they had dwelt on what they had accomplished and figured out, battles fought and terrain gained or lost. Parents themselves, they no longer blamed their own parents for their flaws. They spent literally hours discussing Gregory and Zachary, Gillian and Tessa. Sketching their feelings about their own childhoods and adolescences, their college and graduate carreers, they emphasized who they were now, not who they had once been. Still, they treasured their images of one another as younger, greener souls, as one might treasure faded pictures in a locket.

When they had finished breakfast, Mort put on his glasses, removed the tray, and crawled back into bed.

He said deliberately, "It's like being married, isn't it?"

"Without the children and the trivia," she answered nervously.

"Falling asleep and waking up together."

Nina's heart fluttered arhythmically and her skin prickled. She wondered if she were going to have cardiac arrest, here in bed with Mort. A scandal. She had been hearing lately about women her age dropping dead of heart attacks and strokes, career women like her, with small children and loving men.

Mort said, "We've never discussed it, but we must."

Nina shut her eyes.

"One of our options," he said, as if he were at a faculty meeting, "is to divorce and marry."

Her eyes opened involuntarily, and she held her breath.

"Of course our marriage might very possibly deteriorate into the kind of marriage each of us already has."

Her voice returned. "You're pessimistic?"

"Realistic."

"I've been madly in love before. Not as surely or totally. Nothing like this. But madly, all the same. It reminds me of the line from *Hamlet,* where he's describing his mother's love for his father:

> . . . why, she would hang on him,
> As if increase of appetite had grown
> By what it fed on. . . .

When I was younger, I made the mistake of believing that if I found a man utterly splendid, I'd always find him so. Experience taught me that the madness abates."

"Now who's pessimistic?"

"No. Greedy. I want to hold on to what we have. Unreasonably."

"If we were to marry, the excessiveness, if it is that, would be modified. The sexual obsession would have to abate"—and he smiled—"if we were to survive. I trust it would never disappear, as long as we were together."

His use of the conditional tense brought back her heart palpitations.

"I understand through you," he said, "the romantic notion of finding one's other half."

She grasped his fingers, as they clutched the blue velvet

comforter. "I feel that, too, a kind of Darby and Joan security. Pot snug. But much more. I feel that I've been looking for you. Being with you is like being reunited, as if in some immemorable time we began together and then were separated. Now we're whole again."

"Our two halves fit. I've loved and married and had fine times with my other lovers, but discovering you, who fits, who completes me, is clearly different." He studied her face and said with great tenderness, "But I'm afraid I have to try to let you go."

She had not been expecting it so bluntly and had no answer.

"You'd be better off with David."

"Balls!" she roared, snatching back her hand, making a fist and pounding the bed. "I wouldn't be better off without you. That's the point."

He became stronger. "David can give you and your boys luxury and financial security that you'd never have with me."

"He'll take good care of Greg and Zach, regardless. He's a decent man. And I earn a living wage. I'm not looking to you for financial support. You're not exactly impoverished."

"In comparison to David. . . ."

"You're beyond compare. And you said marriage is one of our options."

"But not now. Only if we can't make our separation work."

"Living separated from you is what's impossible."

"We probably wouldn't be missing so much." He considered. "We'd get bogged down in dailiness. Money worries and disagreements. I'd have to endure your premenstrual tension and your infernal diets."

She took it up: "Living with more than one man means a simple stop at the supermarket becomes a goddamned trip down memory lane. Ale—Nick, imported beer—David, low-calorie beer—Mort; dill pickles—Nick, sweet pickle chips—David, gherkins—Mort; Saltines—Nick, Ritz—David, Triscuits—Mort. And so on, aisle after aisle."

"I'd have to get accustomed to your cooking."

"In the summer, I'd want to go to the mountains and you'd want to go to the beach."

"At Christmas, I'd want to ski and you'd want to snorkel."

"I'd have to cross out all David's clothes' sizes in my notebook and write in yours."

"I'd have to clear your pantyhose out of the shower before I could bathe."

"I'd have to change all the charge accounts."

"I have a dog."

"I have a cat."

"You'd have the TV on when I wanted to listen to records."

"You'd have the TV on when I wanted to read."

"You'd be ready for dinner, and I'd want to relax and have a drink."

"You'd turn the radiators on, and I'd turn them off."

"You'd speak directly to headwaiters instead of leaving that to me."

"You'd miss a cab I could have hailed."

"You'd buy the wrong wine."

"You'd forget to uncork it at the proper time."

"You'd kick me in bed."

"You'd snore."

"You'd be involved with Zach and Greg when I wanted your undivided attention."

"You'd go off with Gillian and Tessa for the day and ignore me."

"You'd be ready for bed, and I'd want to stay up and talk."

"You'd sleep late on weekends when I'd want you to come out and bum around with me."

"You punish by withdrawing."

"You close down when you're scared."

"You talk too fast."

"You're too straight, square."

"You're moody and defensive."

"You're cool and analytical under emotional stress."

"You're too tall."

"You're too short."

He threw back the covers in an obscene gesture and declared, "I'm big for my size!"

They laughed and began to wrestle. When they were breathless, their stress diffused, they resumed their conversation.

"You don't *want* to marry me," Nina challenged. "You're using this opulent opportunity David supposedly offers me as an excuse to opt out."

"Oh, oh, oh."

"It's true."

"I want to marry you more than I've ever wanted anything or anyone. No matter how trivialized our life became, it would be the best that life can be, because we were together."

"Precisely. I was thinking the other day, as I repotted house plants, that your tap root has grown into me and sent out rootlets; to dislodge you would be to destroy us both."

"We don't know that unless we try."

"I don't want to."

"Time mutes."

"I want you more than David. You want me more than Kitty."

"We have children to consider." He got out of bed and put

on his blue plaid robe. "I think I'll light the fire."

She slipped into her amber fleece robe and followed him into the living room. She pushed the armchair up to the fireplace. He sat on the matching footstool, on the other side of the fireplace.

She said, "We'll be better parents, fully alive together, than we will be apart, zombies."

"I acknowledge that we all might be happier in the long run, if you and I marry—the children secure with adults who love as we do, Kitty and David free to find other partners who would appreciate them better than we do. Still, I don't want to deprive you of the kind of life David can now provide for you."

"I can't believe I'm hearing macho pride creep into this discussion. I don't want that life."

"That's the worst part."

Nina said almost coyly, "If we marry, we can both go on working at Twickham. If we get caught having an affair, we probably can't."

"If we marry, we can, naturally, both work at Twickham. We won't be caught having an affair, because we're going to end it."

She squeaked, "When?"

Mort's left eye began to twitch. "Today, I guess."

Nina felt faint.

"We're not getting tired of each other as we'd expected," he said. "We'd hoped that giving in, we'd wear out the attraction."

"What we have is much more substantial than a brief fling. It's real."

"Real. Yes."

"We'll see each other all the time at Twickham."

"We'll hide from each other under thick skins, within thick shells."

"Like lugubrious land tortoises?"

"Exactly."

"We tried that before."

"We hadn't had each other then. We needed to find out. Now we know."

"How wonderful we are together." Nina was nauseated and lightheaded. Her palms and soles were moist.

"Nina, the pain will ease."

"Bullshit. I should never have told you about the apartments."

"You had to tell me. We only have a couple of months before summer vacation. By fall our armor will be secure."

"And if our amour is even more secure?"

"We'll see then."

"A reprieve?"

His brow wrinkled. "Don't look at it that way. We must try to give each other up."

"Why can't we stay together until vacation?"

"Once I've made a decision, I have to act on it."

"I remember. I can tell you this: our 'trial separation' will be a dismal failure."

He looked away, out the window, at the seductive spring day —bright sun, new leaves, chirruping birds. " 'April is the cruelest month.' "

Nina picked up the poker and jabbed at the logs. The top one rolled down onto the hearth. Mort put it back with the tongs and took the poker out of her hand.

"We owe it to our children to try to maintain our present marriages," he said.

"Christ! You sound like a Twickham memo."

He stared into the fire and his eyes filled with tears. Seeing them, she wept.

They never returned to that apartment.

*

Nina would remember the next two months in shades of brown, as if her life had switched from color to a sepia print. She caught a spring cold, which deteriorated into pneumonia. Antibiotics healed her body, but she was out of school for two weeks, and although her classes were unruly after her absence, she was indifferent. In faculty meetings, she aimed her eyes over Mort's head, as he had once told her he had aimed his rifle over the heads of the enemy in Korea. Faculty members gossiped that it was a shame, after such a strong start, that the headmaster was finishing the year in first gear. Nina always changed the subject.

David ceased urging her to look with him at cooperative apartments. He perceived that he must alter his strategy and perhaps must alter his objective as well.

# 17

## COASTING

SHE was waiting for him when he got back to the hotel that warm June afternoon in Beverly Hills. She was standing in the middle of his room, wearing only the bottom of her black bikini bathing suit. Her soaking hair made a dark cap on her head. He heard the shower running in the bathroom.

"I just came in from the pool," she explained. "I was about to rinse off when I heard you at the door."

He tossed his key on the painted white dresser and kissed her, holding his body away from hers so that his new suit did not get wet.

"You're already tan," he observed, surveying her slim, boyish body with admiration. Despite two children, the skin was taut, the small breasts high, the muscles firm. Her rigorous daily exercise routine paid off.

"I've been sunbathing at my sister's, too."

"Without a top. Nice. How was your flight down from San Francisco?"

"Uneventful."

"I wasn't sure you'd come."

"Oh, David, you're impossible. I said I'd join you here."

He removed his shirt and tie. "No trouble at the desk?"

"I said I was Mrs. Lathrop and gave them the room number you'd told me on the phone yesterday. Simple."

"How did it feel being Mrs. Lathrop?"

"Like bigamy. The clerk took in my wedding ring. Mort's wedding ring."

"Do you want a drink?"

"Not now. Thanks. I've got to shower." Kitty disappeared into the bathroom and shut the door behind her.

David poured into a tumbler two fingers of Scotch from the bottle he kept on a round white table beside the sliding glass doors onto the patio. The ice bucket was freshly filled with ice. David knocked on the bathroom door.

"Come in."

"I'm getting water for my drink. Did you have something already? There's ice in the bucket."

"Not yet. I filled it for you."

Kitty interpreted accurately the brief pause before David's "thanks." Nina never made such courtesanlike gestures, considering them beneath her. Kitty began to sing as she soaped.

David arranged the pillows so that he could read The *Wall Street Journal* in bed. He filled and lit his pipe and lay down. He had kept on his white, synthetically silky, French bikini undershorts: they showed off his box. As he was reading and drinking his Scotch, the noise of the shower torrent ceased and a hair dryer began to hum. Eventually, Kitty emerged from the bathroom, wrapped in a pale blue robe, tied loosely at her waist. It was very short. She poured herself a Tab.

"What've you done to your hair?" asked David.

"I had it cut and streaked before I left New York. Like it?" She slid open the glass door and stood enjoying the warm air and the tropical flowers and plants growing on their private patio.

"You look fabulous. Does Mort like it?"

"Said so, but he's been depressed the last couple of months. It's hard to tell."

"So has Nina. Twickham must be going to hell in a basket, if it has that effect."

"Nina's pneumonia depressed her. She was low when I visited her at your place, remember? I took her a bunch of lilacs."

"She gave them to the housekeeper. I think she's jealous of you."

Kitty turned impatiently. "Why on earth would she be? She's married to you."

"She doesn't think that's so great." He did not disguise his sadness.

"Ridiculous." Kitty shut the door, to keep the heat out and the air conditioning in. She stretched beside him on the bed.

"Nina thinks I'm a workaholic, cold and obsessed with business," David said bleakly.

"Nothing is sexier than power, and of course you have to work for that. You look like a movie star, you travel first class, your business is exciting."

"She thinks it's unspeakably boring."

"I love hearing all the show biz intrigue you're privy to with this new client. I didn't know you before you were on the high wire."

"You'll get to participate tonight. We're going to dinner with one of my clients and his wife."

Kitty was both flattered and frightened. "Does he think I'm your wife?"

"I said my wife is at home. I described you as a friend, here on your own business, whom I've asked to join us. He didn't pry. I did explain that you are an artist, were visiting your sister in San

Francisco, and have come here with slides of your work to try to place it in a local gallery. He said his wife may be able to help you."

"Really?"

"You did bring your slides?"

"In my purse. I wouldn't trust them to the airlines in my luggage. Irene gave me her blessing."

Kitty fell silent, and as she thought she became solemn.

"Penny for 'em?"

"Mort and Nina. Maybe they found out about you and me, then, in April, when they both started going downhill? I mean, I didn't notice the rest of the faculty falling apart. I don't think anything at Twickham is the reason."

David folded the newspaper and put it on the bedside table. "Do you sincerely think that?"

"Why not? In New York we may have been seen—going into our hotel, in restaurants or bars."

"I chose those places very carefully, for the unlikelihood of anyone who knows Nina or Mort ever going to them. I'd hate for them to be wounded."

"Still . . ."

"Mort wouldn't tell you, if he knew?"

"He might wait and see if I got over it. He's been going through the motions of marriage, but he's not really with me."

David had let his pipe go out. He lay down and put his arm around Kitty. She rested her head on his shoulder.

He said, "I'm really with you."

"It feels that way."

"You smell, I don't know, inviting. Sexy and expensive."

"It's the new me." Pause. "I love your hairy chest."

"Mort's isn't?"

"It's smooth as a baby's derrière."

Her fingers swirled lazily over his skin, starting at his collar bone and working very slowly downward. Her perfectly manicured nails were painted brownish pink, to hide the pigment that inevitably got beneath them too deeply to be removed. Mort and her parents had all told her that nail polish is vulgar. David liked it.

"Nina would suffer in silence if she found out, that's for sure," David said.

Kitty fingered his nipples delicately. She refrained from saying, "You mean, she always does?" but asked, "Do you think they know we're here together?"

"Jesus! I hope not! But if they know about us, they've figured out that when you visit your sister in San Francisco during a week when I'm in Los Angeles on business, we're not telling them the whole truth."

"No wonder Mort was so distracted about leaving for the Cape. I never wanted to cause him suffering."

"Nina hated moving to Connecticut for the summer, very unlike her."

"What shall we do?"

"Do? You'll join Mort and your girls on the Cape. I'll commute to Nina and my boys in Connecticut. We'll be considerate and affectionate with our mates. You and I will be separated all summer, which won't be easy."

"I mean, should we confess and apologize and promise it will never happen again?" She blew lightly on his brown chest hairs.

"But it will." He kissed the top of her head, noting that the streaking had disguised the scattered grey hairs.

"We can't torture them. They're good people. We've agreed

on that. We have no valid gripes. If they've found us out, we have to stop."

Kitty did not accept, as he did, that their affair was not to be abandoned at will.

"We've outgrown them." David took off his glasses and laid them on top of the *Journal*. "And we've grown together."

Her hand made figure-eights on his abdomen, stopping tactfully at his shorts, avoiding that issue. "We have children to consider."

"That's the sticking place." He reached inside his shorts and rearranged things.

"We don't have to cope with Mort and Nina today," she said.

"Let's not."

*

The Silks collected Kitty and David from their hotel. When they were ensconced in the back seat of their host's white Rolls Royce, David performed the introductions:

"Amelia and Howard Silk, Catherine Myers."

Kitty smiled warmly and said, "I've heard such nice things about you."

Amelia, who had turned around to look at them, said, "That's mutual."

At the restaurant, the *maître d'hôtel* greeted the Silks respectfully and led them to a choice table in the dark, candlelit

room. The design theme was pseudo-Spanish, with much white
stucco, black wrought-iron and dark wood.

Kitty started to sit next to Howard but hesitated, and he said,
"Why don't you sit by Amelia, Catherine?" placing her between
his wife and David.

Kitty thought, "The men sit next to each other, so they can
talk shop, and the women sit next to their own men, so no one
can flirt."

She judged Howard to be in his late fifties. What hair he had
was white, and the top of his bald head was as brown as his face.
He wore a tan suit, pale green shirt, and dark brown tie. Amelia
was a generation younger than her husband—perhaps early thirties. Her palomino hair curled softly around her face and her
chrome-yellow, very slinky and costly dress showed off her tan.
Her makeup was so craftily applied that Kitty had to concentrate
to decipher a plain face beneath it. Kitty thought she was kicky.
No one would mistake her for a teacher or faculty wife. Not that
Kitty appeared to be remotely connected to a private Eastern
school. She wore a turquoise silk dress, which was slit to her waist
in front and in back. She had bought it in San Francisco, and it
was not a look she wanted to explain to Mort. David had said,
when she dressed, that she was perfection.

She wore diamond-stud earrings, which David had presented
to her as they were about to leave their hotel room, making her
quite lightheaded with pleasure. Had he planned to give them to
Nina, if she chickened out and stayed in San Francisco? It was
a shame that she would have to tell Mort that they were fakes that
she had bought for herself, because that would mean discarding
the darling little box from a Beverly Hills jeweler. Kitty pushed
her straight blonde hair behind her ears, to display the earrings,
which delighted David. It was pathetic that a man in his position

was actually grateful if you appreciated the fruits of his labor. Kitty's mother would have conniptions if she could see Kitty now (not like her older sister, who had been encouraging).

David asked Howard to order champagne for her, explaining that "Catherine drinks only champagne."

Amelia agreed to share a bottle of the bubbly, and the men ordered real drinks.

Howard Silk was important to David. Amelia was important to Howard. Amelia apparently knew local art galleries. Kitty went to work. Their perfumes blended, as she leaned slightly toward the younger woman and asked how long she had lived in California. Skillfully, without seeming to ask too many questions, Kitty elicited an autobiographical outline. Before the waiter had plunked into their hands giant menus with fuzzy red covers, she knew that Amelia was Howard's second wife (*"Quelle surprise!"* she said later to David, passing along serviceable tidbits), that they had a seven-year-old daughter, who was in psychoanalysis, and that Howard had grandchildren through his son and two daughters by his first marriage. Amelia, no slouch herself as a helpmeet, managed to find out quite a lot about Kitty's New York life, without once alluding to the father of Gillian and Tessa. It was not for her to make Howard's clever young lawyer's classy mistress feel morally abject.

A trio played, and after dinner, David asked Kitty to dance. The dance floor was miniscule, with approximately two square feet of floor space per couple. Sometimes the music invited partners to touch as they danced and sometimes it suggested separation. David's hand moved from Kitty's dress to her bare back. She was wearing high-heeled sandals, but her face only reached his shoulder.

"You're gloriously tall," she murmured, looking up into his

large, dark eyes and smiling. "There's so much of you, it makes a girl feel very secure."

He squeezed her so tightly that her breasts flattened out against him.

Howard and Amelia were dancing, too. He was a solid man of medium height and impressive posture. He held himself erect, with a naturalness that indicated that he took for granted getting his own way. Amelia was graceful and gay. Her enormous diamond engagement ring glittered on his shoulder, as they swayed in time to the music. Kitty surmised correctly that they four would not exchange dance partners. She could not tell if Howard did not trust David with Amelia or if he did not trust himself with her. Or both of the above. Returning to their table, they ordered brandy and Perrier water. Howard engaged Kitty in small talk, and she was charming and circumspect.

"I always think of Boston as a young city," Howard was saying, after he had asked where she grew up. His hand knocked over his cup of espresso, which the waiter had refilled. The deep brown stain spread out irregularly on the white tablecloth. "It's all right, it absorbs quickly." He folded the fabric up along the edge of the table, making a linen dam.

Kitty pretended to ignore the accident, but she felt it revealed more than what he was saying. He seemed satisfied with her and shifted his attention to David once again. As Kitty pondered how to broach the subject of art galleries to Amelia, Amelia asked if she had any free time the next day?

"All day," Kitty responded candidly. "David will be working."

"Would you like to see the shops?"

"Adore to."

"I'll pick you up at noon. Look for a white Mercedes coupe.

The Rolls is Howard's. We'll have lunch first."

Amelia, almost self-effacingly, asked, "Howard thought you might have slides of your work? I know a few gallery owners. Howard and I collect. Would you'd like to meet them? They're always on the lookout for new talent. Howard has seen your paintings in David's office, and he says you're important."

"Why, thank you. That would be darling of you." So Howard had connected her with David's paintings. Sharp.

"We're set then, love," said Amelia.

*

Kitty and David got ready for bed quickly. Kitty boiled her soft contact lenses and put on her new, mauve, Empire-style nightgown. David wore sleek beige pajamas. They sat on their patio, David smoking his pipe.

"You really worked tonight," he said. "I want you to know I appreciate that."

"Nina never goes on business trips with you?"

"She can't get away from Twickham."

"This is fun. It's too bad she has to give it up."

"She'd hate it."

"What's to hate?"

"Nina would find the hotel sinfully expensive . . ."

"It is that."

"The restaurant pretentious and vulgar, and the Silks shallow."

"What's her idea of fun?"

"I wish I knew."

"Well, I'm enchanted."

"You're an asset."

He sounded sad and lonely. Kitty knew he was wishing that he had a wife like her (her for a wife?), as she was wishing that her husband led his life.

"This hotel is soothing," said Kitty. "Mort and I can't afford luxury accommodations. Money does buy happiness, doesn't it?"

"Nina says the opposite."

"If you have health, a satisfying career, and decent human relationships, money buys about everything else."

"Nina's opinion is that money and decent human relationships are mutually exclusive."

"She confuses the quantity of time spent together with its quality."

"Does she?" He liked that interpretation. Kitty made life easier.

Kitty expounded. "I had a happy time with you tonight, although we hardly spoke. You and Howard talked business, while Amelia and I got acquainted. Yet you and I were together"—she laughed—"hustling with verve, eating well, and drinking fine wines."

"That's the way I feel," he said gloomily, meditating upon his marriage.

"If my husband traveled the way you do and wanted me to go along, I'd go."

"You made a hit with the Silks. You really won over Amelia."

"She was on guard at first, I guess because I paint and she doesn't have a career. Except for being Howard's wife, which I'll bet keeps her busy."

"She was afraid you'd look down on her?"

"How can I look down on someone who has her own Mercedes coupe?"

"Baby, you fit right in out here. But if you did this regularly, it would kill you professionally."

"Nonsense. It's a terrific release from painting. I see everything—the bodies, the light, the vegetation—as an artist. I'm storing it away. I sketch and photograph. I was sketching today, before I swam."

"Doesn't this superficial wheeling and dealing corrupt you?"

"The tension is useful," she assured him.

"How can you be so beautiful and talented and still fill the ice bucket?" he asked plaintively.

"I don't fill ice buckets for just anyone."

He stood and reached for her in the dark, pulling her into his arms and holding her, smelling her fragrant hair. Then they went to bed, curling up like spoons, as if they belonged, hardly believing that this was their first night sleeping in the same bed.

# 18

# FLIGHT

KITTY and David breakfasted on their patio, surrounded by colorful exotic plantings.

"Another shitty day in Paradise," said he.

"The weather is heavenly."

"I have a surprise for you." He took out his thick wallet and laid fifteen hundred-dollar bills, one at a time, on the table between them.

"What's that?"

"Pocket money for your spree with Amelia."

Kitty was shocked. "You must be kidding!"

"I never kid about money."

She glared at him. "You may find this peculiar, under the circumstances, but I'm not that kind of girl."

"Don't go conventional on me. I'm not implying that you're a hooker." He laughed at the absurdity.

"What are you implying?"

"That you understand me well enough to know that I get a boost out of making money and that I'm sick of not having anyone who will enjoy spending it. That you care enough about me to accept this loving gift."

Kitty thought of Nina's disgust at the idea of a new mink

coat, her refusal to buy a cooperative apartment, her dull endurance during dinners with his clients.

She said, "What a bind. My entire upbringing says, no, no, . . ."

"But there's yes, yes, in your eyes."

"I have a bit of my own money, you know. A modest portfolio, thanks to my parents. Mort insists we live mostly on his income, but I will be able to lay hands on fifteen hundred dollars of my own and pay you back. I admit I'd have fun spending it today. I've always wanted to."

"To break loose?"

"If you will."

"But, dearest, I want you to spend *my* money. I can't give it all to charity and to my sons. Fifteen hundred isn't that much."

"It's a fortune to spend in boutiques, at least it is for me."

He seemed to shrink in his chair. His hair was greying slightly at the temples, giving him distinction. He must not be allowed to feel discouraged, he must be aggressive and self-confident. Kitty had come to see him as one of the most vulnerable men she had known.

"Look," she said, "I'll take the money happily and, when we get home, we'll decide about my paying it back."

He regarded her unsmilingly.

"You're younger than I," she teased. "Trust me."

"Nearly three long years. I look older."

"Do you mind the difference?"

"Older women, with their experience and know-how, have always attracted me. You have all the advantages without the disadvantages."

"Meaning advanced wrinkles."

"And crêpey skin."

"Time will take its toll one day."

"You'll always be pretty. You have the bone structure."

"Blarney." Kitty picked up the wad of bills and tucked them ostentatiously under her robe, into the bodice of her nightgown. They bulged. "Drop by whenever you like," she said in a sultry low register.

"I wish I didn't have to go, but I have an appointment."

"See you tonight, then."

When they kissed, David slipped his hand inside her robe, fondling her breast and the bills simultaneously.

"Philistine," she called after him as he went indoors. "And it's all a big front," she added softly to herself.

\*

Amelia figured out that Kitty would be a more amusing shopping companion, if the question of a gallery were settled. She telephoned several gallery owners, arranging for appointments after lunch. By three in the afternoon, Kitty had a Los Angeles outlet for her paintings. As prearranged with Irene Martell, who would be taking a percentage of Kitty's West Coast sales, Kitty and her new California representative telephoned Irene in New York. The two gallery owners worked out the technicalities.

"I'm indebted to you," Kitty told Amelia later. "If there's ever anything I can do for you . . ."

"Be good to David, love."

Kitty removed her sunglasses, as if that would improve her hearing.

"I'm serious," said Amelia. "I'm going to be up front with you."

Kitty was not convinced that she was ready for this. They were sitting in a cheerful green-and-white café, over giant goblets filled with freshly blended fruit drinks. There was a bowl of roasted sunflower seeds on the table, from which they nibbled.

"I haven't met David's wife." Amelia forged ahead. "Howard says she's—to be blunt—a drag. No help at all to his career."

Kitty lowered her eyes to hide her unbecoming elation at the course this lecture was taking. Amelia was a decade younger than she but not less knowing.

"I've been making up my mind all day about whether to speak to you," Amelia continued. "I decided I can trust you. I wouldn't want any of this to get back to David and Howard. It's girl talk. Okay?"

Kitty nodded, still not looking at her. She was amazed by how much she wanted to hear exactly what Amelia was now saying:

"Howard was really tickled when they found David. He says he's extremely smart at what he does. Then he met his wife in New York, and his reaction was hostile. She's cold and superior, and she doesn't support him or know how to dress. Not that she'll harm David's career. He's making it without her. But now that I've met him, I can see that he deserves better. He deserves a wife who will be behind him." Inexplicably, her eyes misted. "You must be like a dream to him. Last night, Howard said, 'Why doesn't he marry her? She has it all.' "

Kitty watched Amelia quizzically.

"You're not Catholic or anything?" Amelia asked.

"I'm Episcopalian, more or less. I don't know what David is. He's not Catholic."

"So you can get divorced."

"He hasn't asked me."

"He will."

"I don't know."

"You wouldn't be here if your own marriage was working."

"How do you know I'm not divorced? This wedding ring could be a ruse."

"You don't act divorced. Are you?"

"No."

"Well?"

Kitty laughed nervously. "Amelia, I really appreciate your intentions, but I don't know what to say. It's embarrassing."

"It's none of my business?"

Kitty shook her head. "I'm grateful for what you're trying to do."

"Let's hit the boutiques."

"Great."


As Kitty pivoted in front of a three-way mirror, appraising the fit of an Ultra-suede coat-dress, Amelia said, "They're surrounded by beautiful women."

"Who?"

"Men in this business. You can't be the jealous type."

"It's purely Platonic, with the broads?"

Amelia replied stoically, "Not necessarily. The temptations are overwhelming. They're not supposed to make it with anyone you have to see."

"Do they all screw around?" Kitty decided to take the dress.

"No, but they all have lots of contact with gorgeous girls who try to seduce them. They have appointments, lunches, out-of-town dinners."

"There are other men in my life, too. If David carried on like that, I'd accept the invitations from old friends who are in New York on business, without their wives. I'll go to shows with artists I know."

"Gay?"

"Not necessarily."

"You'd go to bed with them?"

"Only if I wanted to, and I knew David were sleeping around."

"It doesn't drive you wild? Is your present marriage like that?"

"Nothing. My husband is faithful. He wouldn't know how to deceive me. This thing with David is the only affair I've ever had." She grinned. "I'm not that kind of person."

Amelia grinned. "None of us are. Howard was married when I met him. Separated, but not planning divorce."

"I'd never marry a man unless I believed totally that he wouldn't cheat."


Stroking the real silk underwear that she was purchasing for Gillian and Tessa, as it lay on the glass counter, Kitty concocted explanations for Mort, about her new loot.

"They're never home," said Amelia. "It's not a private life they want so much as the appearance of a private life."

"Husbands?"

"They work late at night, over holidays, on weekends. You can't be the dependent type who's scared to be alone."

"I have a full life of my own."

"You're lucky you have your art."

"Do you get bored?"

"Not anymore. I'm taking acting lessons."


Kitty was trying to decide between two wallets for David. It bothered her that his was so worn. The one in her left hand was black lizard. The one in her right hand was soft and felt like— what? She shut her eyes and concentrated on the sensation in her fingertips: the head of his penis, that's what the leather felt like.

"I'll take this one," she announced, holding out her right hand, relishing the sybaritic pleasure she was giving him.

As an afterthought, she bought a lizard glasses case for Mort.

"They don't spend enough time with their children," said Amelia. "You can't be the type who won't play father, too, and cover for him with excuses."

"My children are nearly in college and I have no intention of having more. Their own father is devoted to them. They don't need a stepfather."

"You're home free," Amelia declared with finality.


*


When David unwrapped his gift wallet, he was gleeful. He sat fingering it while Kitty displayed her other purchases. She realized that she really was in love with him. He dropped his old wallet into the wastebasket, and she wondered if Nina had given it to him.

Before they left California, David and Kitty sent to the Silks a case of Roederer Cristal Champagne.

"Nina brought home a bottle on impulse one evening, and it's delicate and aristocratic," David explained to Kitty. "The Silks will like it, as a change from the usual."

"I know it well," said Kitty. "It's Mort's favorite."

David frowned. "Perhaps the subject of champagne came up one day in the faculty lounge."

"Perhaps." Kitty felt a buzz at the back of her mind, a tingling along the hairs of her forearms.

"I'm all ready and packed," she said.

\*

Kitty and David flew first-class back to New York. Nina sneered at first class, preferring tourist, but Kitty appreciated being pampered. As soon as the No Smoking sign went off, David lit his pipe (the unvarnished briar pipe he took whenever he traveled, because it was his favorite).

"We're going to get married," he said.

Kitty spluttered over her champagne. "Who says?"

"It goes almost without saying. We belong together, proverbial hand in proverbial glove. Hadn't you noticed?"

"Now that you mention it. But seriously, David, what about our children?"

"We'll buy a brownstone with enough bedrooms so each of the four can have one. You'll have a studio on the top floor. We'll put in skylights or whatever you need. Your daughters will live with us. We'll hire a housekeeper. My sons will live with their mother, and she'll keep our present housekeeper. They'll spend as much time with us as possible. I assume that Mort will arrange time with Gillian and Tessa. He seems conscientious."

"You've thought it all out."

"Of course."

"Your boys are awfully young."

"I hope that Nina will remarry, for their sake, as well as for hers."

"Do you think she will?"

"Somehow I don't doubt it."

"I accept."

"What?"

"I merely mentioned that I accept your proposal of marriage."

He kissed her as romantically as was comfortable in so public a place. People watched them when they were together. Amelia had explained: "You're a striking couple. That's a turnon."

Outside the little window, the sky was a brilliant blue that reminded Kitty of the Virgin's gown in the Portinari altarpiece. As a young art student in Florence, she had stood before that Nativity, soaking in the astonishing hue. It was such a long time ago that she had flown to and from Italy on a propeller plane.

"This never would have happened, if I hadn't lost Mort to Twickham," she said.

"Nina evaporated on me, too."

"It wasn't that I saw less of him, although I did, it was that a crevasse slowly opened between us. I tried to bridge it. I can't reach him. He seems sober and earnest and, well, young, although he's older than I. I've changed tremendously but he's still idealistic and dedicated to children. I like kids, but enough is enough."

"I'll say. It's funny, the way you put it, it sounds like a description of Nina and me."

"We tried."

"It's best to make a clean break, for them, too. Do you want the summer to reconsider?"

Kitty thought, "Forty-two is young enough, but it's not exactly younger than springtime." And how could she and David face a long hot summer of separation? She said, "I'm positive," and she removed Mort's wedding ring and dropped it into her pocketbook. "Making tough decisions can save your life, but they don't get easier. *Avanti.*"

"I failed, a moment ago, to include that I love you. You're superlative, on canvas and on percale. In every way."

She took his hand. "I love and admire you very much, and you're the sexiest man I've ever known." She kept to herself that in bed Mort was too athletic for her and too soulful.

"How do you think Mort and Nina will take our news?" she asked.

"They will be very surprised."

"Do you think they'll collapse?"

David responded with more certainty than he had realized he felt, "We don't need to worry about them. Maybe they'll even be happy to be free. Life is full of surprises. I feel we're doing the right thing for everyone."

Kitty and David smiled and clinked their champagne glasses together in a silent toast. The airplane began to level off, having ascended smoothly to its cruising altitude.

# 19

⊰⟡⟡⟡⊱

# CONFRONTATION

TELLING Mort was not going to be easy. Kitty still hadn't decided how to launch the subject when she arrived at their summer house on Cape Cod. The champagne she had drunk on the plane muddled her thoughts, but she was aware of the contrast between the luxury of Beverly Hills and the plain simplicity of this small house. There, everything had been done for her. Here, she was her own housekeeper. There, her main man was David. Here, he was Mort. In both places, Kitty felt like a visitor. Mort greeted her with surface warmth but seemed distant. She had to tell him before Gillian and Tessa returned from the movies. "Just get it over with," she muttered.

Kitty changed to blue cotton slacks and a brown T-shirt and unpacked, slowly putting away her clothes, stalling for time. As she did this, she decided how she must inform her husband.

When she joined Mort in the living room, he brought her a mug of coffee, saying, "I thought you might need this."

"You noticed that I'd been drinking on the plane."

"When I kissed you."

Kitty drew shut the draperies and curled up on the window seat. Mort sat in a wingback armchair covered in flowered chintz

201

and put his feet on the wood coffee table, facing Kitty from across the room.

"I became so involved in conversation with the person next to me on the plane that I didn't notice how freely the champagne flowed."

"A fascinating seatmate."

"A woman. You would have liked her, I think. She's in the midst of a personal crisis."

"And she confided in you."

"She has decided to ask her husband for a divorce, and she was having a hard time seeing how best to do it, because their marriage had disintegrated so quietly, so gently, that they hadn't noticed until it was over."

"How inattentive of them." He pushed his tortoise-shell glasses higher on the bridge of his nose.

"You see, her husband drifted out of her life in all but the most perfunctory ways, and then she met a man who couldn't help wanting to be with her."

"Does she want to be with him?"

"They were thrown together because of her work. He was one of her clients."

Mort removed his feet from the coffee table.

"And he remained only that?"

"They became lovers."

Mort thought before asking, "Are there children?"

"Teenagers."

"Hers or his?"

"Hers are teenagers. His are younger."

"He's still married?"

"He's getting divorced, too."

"A lover is insufficient reason to destroy two families," Mort declared stiffly.

"A lifeless marriage combined with a lover is a pretty strong reason, I'd say."

Kitty leaned over and set her empty coffee mug on the floor, then sat back, hugging her knees.

Mort avoided her eyes as he asked, "What's so terrible about her marriage?"

"Her husband lost interest in her. They rarely make love, and sex is important to her. He tolerates her career and minimizes her talent. The man with whom she has realigned encourages her career and admires her. He loves making love to her. She feels important with him and inconsequential with her husband."

Kitty watched while her words dredged from Mort's unconscious knowledge what had been hidden there for some time. They were immobile.

He said sadly, "Did he give her diamond earrings?"

Kitty guiltily fingered the sparkling studs. "I'm sorry. I didn't want this to happen. I have to feel connected. I can't live in the detached style you've developed since we moved to New York."

Mort waited for her to look directly at him before asking, "Do I know him?"

"You can't blame him. He treasures my paintings. He buys them. He's been responsible for other people buying them. His wife is cold and patronizing."

Mort's eyes dimmed and his mouth slackened.

Kitty continued. "We make each other happy, and we can't do that for our mates, no matter how hard we try."

Mort said with a ferocity that frightened her, "Tell me his name."

"You've guessed."

"You tell me."

"David."

"Lathrop?"

"David Lathrop."

"You're planning to marry."

"That's right. We are."

Mort stared at her, unblinking. In that instant, his face became unrecognizable. Was this the man she had been married to all these years? She peered at him, trying to find her husband. The silence went on too long.

"Mort?" she whispered. "Are you there?"

He only stared.

"Are you in shock?" she asked abruptly.

"In April, you and David," he said.

"What?"

"Were sleeping together."

She laughed uneasily. "Not exactly sleeping."

"Fucking."

That was not a word she had ever before heard Mort use. She was afraid to speak.

"You were fucking David in April? And May? And now June. All those lost months."

"Lost?"

"Am I correct?"

Kitty had no idea what he was talking about, but she replied steadily, "The affair began early this year."

"And continued unabated?"

"Well, naturally, we . . ."

"Naturally? It never occurred to you to separate? To give each other up for your children and for Nina and me?"

There was something odd, Kitty noticed, in the way Mort

pronounced, "Nina and me;" his voice rose in pitch and tightened.

"Not seriously. We want to stay together, frankly."

"It's unbelievable that you're being this cavalier about your
daughters. You ought to show human concern for those little
Lathrop boys, too. Egomaniacal. You're *egomaniacal*!"

"I deserve a life of my own. The way David has it planned,
the children will live very well. Don't be so goddamned sanc-
timonious."

Mort shook his head and Kitty continued defensively. "We
realized on this trip to California—we met in Beverly Hills, after
I visited my sister—that it will work best for everyone, children
included, if we're married to each other."

"I hope so. I hope it's not too late."

"Too late for what?"

Mort screamed at her for the first and last time. "*What if
Nina had died in May of her pneumonia?*"

"He's crazy," thought Kitty. "I've driven him crazy."

"We can discuss it later," she said soothingly.

"Why didn't we discuss it sooner?"

Kitty's face went blank.

"Why didn't you tell me earlier? In April?"

He sounded sane. Furious but sane.

"What's so special about April?" Kitty asked in exasperation.

"April is when I gave up Nina."

Comprehension spread over Kitty's face, starting in her eyes
and ending on her lips in a grin.

"You bastard," she said. "You bastard." It was the only word
she could think of, and she spoke it with as much appreciation
as dismay.

Mort stood up and went to the front door, opening it and standing with his back to her, listening to the waves break on the shore and breathing cool sea air.

Kitty did not know what they were supposed to talk about next. The momentum that had kept her going since David's marriage proposal terminated with Mort's oblique confession.

"All the time I thought you loved me," she said, "you were loving her."

"In a different way. I'm in love with her."

"You and I. We haven't been in love for quite awhile."

"We once were."

"I don't know where it goes. It's frightening how unreliable love is."

Mort came over and perched on the other end of the window seat, opposite Kitty. "Our romance began when we were young and saw in each other what we wanted to find."

"Maybe we made unconscious adjustments. Maybe David and Nina are fantasy figures to you and me, too."

"Maybe . . . maybe we're able to see more clearly and are more accepting than when we met."

Kitty said wistfully, "Our marriage wasn't a failure."

"I wouldn't have missed it."

"You don't wish you'd met Nina instead of me, right at the start, except for Gillian and Tessa?"

"Nina and I probably wouldn't have liked each other back then."

"I'm glad." She was silent for a moment before saying, "We'll keep in touch, because of the girls. And because we want to."

"I'll miss you."

"Only at first. Is David telling Nina tonight?"

"That was our agreement."

Mort looked at his watch. "Then she knows. I'm going to phone her."

\*

David and Nina sat looking up at the twinkling night sky. Their sons were already asleep when David got home. He had left his suitcase beside the front door and led Nina by the hand out onto the deck, removing his jacket and tie before sitting down in one of the webbed aluminum chairs.

Nina was too thin, and her faded cotton sundress hung on her loosely.

"Nina," David began, "I have something very serious and difficult to tell you."

He was using his lawyer's voice, and she wondered if the conglomerate had fired him.

"In the beginning, it will be painful, but we'll find, I'm sure, that in the long run, our lives will be happier." He paused to recall what else he had planned to say.

"He's been canned," thought Nina. "Maybe there's hope. He'll become more human."

"You and I have to consider the boys and how to make this as easy as possible for them."

Nina thought, "So they won't each have a new bedroom. They don't mind sharing a room too much."

"I'll always take care of you," said David. "I want you to feel confident about that and not to worry."

"I know that." She smiled supportingly, her face lit by a lamp inside the window.

"Nina, I have to say it right out. I want a divorce."

Nina jerked to full attention. "Divorce? What the hell for?"

David, taken aback, answered more candidly than he had intended at this point in their conversation. "So I can marry Catherine Myers."

For Nina, the picture came into focus, the outlines clear, the colors intense. "Kitty Hinks."

"Exactly."

Nina jumped out of her chair with a joyful whoop and flung herself into David's lap, kissing him energetically on the mouth. He responded out of habit; then he became confused and, fearing that her intention was to convince him, through seduction, to change his mind, he turned away his head.

Nina stood and beamed down on him. "Does Mort know?"

Irritated by her irrational cheerfulness, he answered sharply, "How should I know?"

"Was Kitty going to tell him tonight?"

"She said so."

"Fabulous."

"Nina, what's the matter with you?"

Nina sat down again, pulling her light aluminum chair closer to his. "Now it's my turn, David dearest."